CANTERWOOD CREST

BEHIND THE BIT

 JESSICA BURKHART

m!x

ALADDIN MIX

New York London Toronto Sydney

m!x

ALADDIN MIX

Simon & Schuster Children's Publishing Division

1230 Avenue of the Americas, New York, NY 10020

Copyright © 2009 by Jessica Burkhart

All rights reserved, including the right of reproduction
in whole or in part in any form.

ALADDIN PAPERBACKS, ALADDIN MIX, and related logo are registered
trademarks of Simon & Schuster, Inc.

Designed by Jessica Handelman

The text of this book was set in Venetian 301 BT.

Manufactured in the United States of America

First Aladdin Paperbacks edition May 2009

14 16 18 20 19 17 15 13

Library of Congress Control Number 2009922881

ISBN: 978-1-4169-5842-0

0115 OFF

ACKNOWLEDGMENTS

Thank you to Alyssa Henkin for your agent-y awesomeness. Can you believe we're on book three?!

Thanks to everyone at Simon & Schuster, especially Jessica Handelman, Lucille Rettino, Venessa Williams, and Nicole Russo.

Monica Stevenson, thank you for snapping the gorgeous cover photo.

Blog readers and friends, thanks so much for putting up with me and for sharing my enthusiasm about Canterwood.

Finally, *Behind the Bit* would be nothing without my super-talented editor, Kate Angelella. TYVM 4 being The. Best. Editor. Ever. I've learned so much from you, and you inspire me to work harder!

Read all of the books in the Canterwood Crest series:

Take the Reins

Chasing Blue

Behind the Bit

For Alyssa Henkin,
I'm so grateful that you searched
for those three magic words!

I

IT'S OVER

I NEVER THOUGHT I'D BE *THIS* GIRL. THE GIRL caught between two guys. The girl who stood outside on a rainy Valentine's Day evening and had no idea what to do. Jacob, my first almost-boyfriend, had just slammed the ballroom door in my face. Eric, my friend and *not at all* boyfriend, took even breaths beside me. But that was Eric. Calm and comforting—like he'd been all night, throughout this horrible mess.

My roommate Paige and I had been sooo excited when we'd stepped into the school's ballroom earlier tonight for the annual seventh and eighth grade Sweetheart Soirée. Now, everything was ruined.

Raindrops bounced off my shoulders and pinged against the sidewalk. The temperature had dropped and the rain was beginning to change to sleet. I couldn't look away from the door. He *had* to come back.

"Sasha?" Eric asked.

"Jacob's not coming back," I whispered. "I messed up everything!"

"Don't say that. C'mon, let's get you inside. I'll walk you back to Winchester."

I finally tore my eyes away from the door and looked at Eric. Concern clouded his dark brown eyes and I realized, just then, how I must have looked. My once-pretty pink dress, now half-covered by Eric's coat, was drenched with rain. My hair, which had been shiny, blow-dried straight, and perfect was now dripping and frizzed at the ends. I didn't even want to imagine how my face looked—probably puffy, red, and streaked with makeup.

Part of me wanted to stand here until Jacob realized that he needed to hear my apology. But the other part—the rational part—*knew* Jacob wouldn't walk through that door again after the way I'd just accused him.

"Okay," I said, nodding numbly. "Let's go."

Eric put an arm around my shoulders as we walked down the slippery sidewalk. I wiped the cold moisture from my face and tried to hold back tears.

"When we get back to your dorm, I'm going to ask your

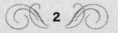

dorm monitor if I can stay. Just until Paige gets back."

I wanted to thank him, to apologize for ruining his night, too, but I couldn't say anything. My brain felt fuzzy and overwhelmed.

Eric steered me toward Winchester Hall, cutting across the slick grass.

Up ahead, two figures passed by under the streetlamp. The sleet blurred their faces, but as we got closer I saw that it was a couple holding hands. Crazy as it was, I still half-expected it to be Heather and Jacob.

"Isn't that—" Eric started.

My breath stopped in my throat and I looked at Eric, wide-eyed.

Heather, holding hands with Ben. Julia's Ben. Julia, as in Heather's best friend. Fifteen minutes ago, Heather had been tormenting me about Jacob. She'd had me convinced that *they* liked each other and that they'd even kissed. She'd obviously moved on already—to breaking up Julia and Ben. But that was what Heather Fox did, wasn't it? I should have known better by now.

I almost laughed out loud, but I didn't even have the energy. Fighting with my friends had exhausted me. In that moment, I couldn't stand to look at Heather for one more second. Eric's arm tightened around me. I raised my

head as we passed Heather and Ben and forced myself not to look at them. Eric did the same.

We walked the final distance to Winchester. Eric opened the door and we stepped inside. I let the warmth of the dorm wash over me, shaking the rainwater off Eric's jacket as I walked. Livvie, the Winchester dorm monitor, poked her head out of her office.

"Sasha! What are you doing bringing a boy in here?" she asked, walking toward us and folding her arms across her chest. "You know the rules—" Her mouth closed when she got a better look at my face. "What happened? Are you all right?"

"I'm fine," I lied. "Can we talk about it later?"

Livvie nodded. "But you're soaked! You should get into dry clothes before you catch cold. I just lit a fire in the common room—why don't you go in there and get warm."

Eric cleared his throat. "Um, I'm Eric," he said. "I'm a friend of Sasha's. Would it be okay if I wait with her until her roommate gets back?"

Livvie looked at me and then at Eric. "Okay, but just until Paige returns. And you're to sit on separate couches. I'll be checking."

I was too tired to be embarrassed, or even laugh. But Eric seemed to think it was funny.

4

"Okay." Eric laughed. "Thanks."

Livvie put her hand on my elbow. "Come find me if you need to talk, okay?"

"'Kay," I whispered. "Thanks, Livvie."

Livvie pointed Eric in the direction of the common room and I headed for my dorm room to change. Once inside, I left the lights off and sat on the edge of my bed. I waited for a fresh wave of tears, but none came. Just numbness. I remembered that Eric was waiting for me. I was so glad—I didn't want to be alone.

Ten minutes later, I'd pulled my damp hair into a sloppy ponytail, shed Eric's jacket, and hung my rain-soaked clothes over the back of my desk chair to dry. I tugged on a soft gray velour hoodie and matching pants and scrounged up a pair of fuzzy pink socks for extra warmth.

The hallway was empty and quiet as I walked back to the common room. I realized that everyone on my floor was still at the Soirée.

When I returned, Eric was standing at the counter, swirling spoons inside two steaming blue mugs.

"Hey," he said, his tone soft. "I made us some hot chocolate."

"Good idea," I said, sitting down on the couch. "I'm still trying to get warmed up."

I tried my best to conjure up a smile for Eric as he set a mug down on the table in front of me.

"I'll sit *way* at the end of this one," Eric said, choosing the couch that sat perpendicular to the one I was on. "I'm afraid an alarm will go off if we sit on the same one."

"It might." I almost laughed. I took a sip of my cocoa and Eric did the same.

For a few minutes, neither of us spoke. We stared at the fireplace across from the couch I was sitting on and watched as a log crackled and turned to ash. The flames cast dancing shadows on the eggshell-colored walls of the room. I drew my feet onto the beige couch and nestled against the arm, finally beginning to absorb the fire's warmth.

"How could I have been so stupid?" I said finally, burying my face in my hands.

"Hey, you're not stupid," Eric said. "Anyone would have believed Heather. I haven't known her very long, but she seems pretty good at causing trouble."

"She is, but I still should have known better. Jacob would never kiss her. He'd never hurt me that way. I should have trusted *him*, but no. I HAD to listen to Heather! And now, he's never going to talk to me again. Jacob hates me and *Callie's* mad at me because . . ." I looked at Eric and

caught myself. "Because," I improvised, "of something that isn't even true. And Paige isn't here yet!"

Oops. I'd just spilled my guts to poor Eric, who was probably ready to bolt for the door by now. Like he'd wanted to hear any of that!

"Sorry," I said. "That was TMI."

Eric smiled, shaking his head. "You're upset. You're allowed to rant, you know."

"Eric, what should I do?" I asked. "Go find Jacob tomorrow and apologize? What if he won't listen?"

"All you can do is try. If he doesn't let you explain, then it's his problem. He should at least give you a chance."

I took a deep breath and let it out, slowly.

"Okay, maybe you're right. I'll try."

"Good." Eric got up from the couch and went back to the kitchen. He opened the cabinet doors and pulled out a bag.

"What's that?" I asked.

"Forgot the marshmallows," he said.

He offered me the bag and I immediately flashed back to my last time at the Sweet Shoppe—our on-campus café/bakery—with Jacob. He knew how much I loved marshmallows and he'd spooned his into my mug when I'd finished mine.

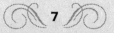

A new wave of tears fell from my eyes. Eric, with a glance at the door for Livvie, stepped across the room and sat beside me.

"Hey," he said, gently. "Did I miss something? Do you hate marshmallows that much?" His jet-black hair fell over one eye as he gazed at me with genuine concern.

"No," I said. "They just . . . bring back some serious Jacob memories."

"Oh. Sorry."

"You didn't know." I sniffled and tried not to start what Oprah called "the ugly cry"—the one with mascara tracks, red eyes, and a Rudolph-bright nose.

"Let me take those." Eric plucked the bag from my hand. "And I'll find another snack, okay?"

I took more deep breaths and blew my nose while Eric looked through the cabinets and tried to find something that wouldn't remind me of Jacob.

"So, I've got a problem with Luna," Eric said. He found a bag of baked chips and poured them into a bowl.

"You do?" I sat up straighter on the couch. "What's wrong?" Eric had listened to me enough—the least I could do was try to help with Luna.

Eric put the bowl on the coffee table between the couches and sat across from me.

"She wants to canter back to the stable after every lesson. I almost can't hold her back from running right into her stall."

"Uh-oh. She's getting barn sour."

"Barn sour?"

I nodded and plucked a chip from the bowl. "If you let her hurry back to the stable after a lesson, she'll always rush. You have to *make* her walk back. If she gets headstrong, circle her until she calms down."

Eric smiled.

"Don't let her rush through a lesson just to get back to her cozy stall. The more eager she is to go back, the farther away you need to lead her. You have to be in charge."

"Good idea. I'll try it." Eric picked up a chip and munched. "Where did you learn that?"

"When I was ten, my parents got me this giant guide book to horses. I read it every—" I stopped and looked at Eric. "You're trying to distract me with horse talk."

"Is it working?"

"Yes," I said, laughing. "It totally is."

"Good. What else was in that book?" He leaned back on the couch as if preparing to be there a while.

"Well . . ."

*

About an hour later, Paige burst into the common room. Her fair cheeks were bright pink and strands of her red hair were plastered to her face.

"Sasha, oh my God, I'm sorry it took me forever to get here!" She yanked off her coat and hurried over to me.

"It's okay," I said. "Eric's been keeping me company."

Paige saw Eric on the other couch and her eyes widened. "Wow, you must have bribed Livvie—big time. Thanks for staying."

"No problem," Eric said, standing. "Sasha's been giving me good horse pointers. But I'll go before Livvie tosses me out into a snow drift or something."

"Thanks for staying," I said. And I meant it. Eric was a good friend. I was overwhelmingly grateful that he'd managed to distract me with questions about Luna. For a few minutes, I'd almost forgotten about Jacob.

Eric tossed me a smile and disappeared through the door.

"C'mon," Paige said, grabbing my hand and pulling me off the couch. "Let's go."

Back in our room, I climbed into bed while Paige took off her makeup and changed into pajamas. It was her fave winter pair—the fuzzy white ones dotted with pink and blue snowflakes. She grabbed a pillow off her bed and

plopped it down next to me. I scooted over and made room for her. She looked at my desk and her eyes landed on something.

"Is that Eric's coat?" she asked.

"Oh, yeah, I wore it back here and completely forgot to give it back. I'll give it to him tomorrow."

Paige scooted closer. "Want to talk?"

I considered telling her about everything I was feeling—missing Jacob, hating myself for believing Heather, and worrying about my friendship with Callie—but it all still felt too raw.

"I just can't go through it again right now. Rain check?" My body was wiped, but my brain wouldn't shut off. It kept replaying the Soirée over and over.

"Deal. Want me to tell you about Headmistress Drake's announcement?" Paige asked.

"Oh, Paige!" I sat up in the bed. "I'm so sorry I didn't ask. Tell me everything." In all of the chaos, I'd forgotten to ask her how the announcement had gone. I'd wanted to be there for the announcement about Paige's gig as the new host of *Teen Cuisine*—the hottest cooking show on The Food Network for Kids.

And so, just like Eric had preoccupied me with horse questions, Paige launched into a second-by-second

detailing of the announcement part of the Soirée. I concentrated on the comforting lull of my friend's voice and pushed away the two images that had been haunting me since I'd left the Canterwood ballroom—the look on Callie's face when she left me with Eric, and the look on Jacob's face when he did the same.

But they were wrong. They both were. And, as I drifted off to sleep, I vowed to myself that I would prove that to them both.

2

SHUT UP AND GET ON YOUR HORSE

BY THE TIME SATURDAY MORNING ROLLED around, I was going stir-crazy in my room. On Friday, we'd only had a half day of classes, and after that, I'd hid in Winchester the rest of the day. It had been bad enough when Callie, my former best friend, had ignored me during English. But then later, in the hallway, Jacob handed me my coat, which I'd accidentally left at the Soirée, and walked off without a word.

Now, most of the other students who attended Canterwood Crest Academy—one of the most exclusive boarding schools on the East Coast—had already jetted home for midwinter break.

This year, the teachers had a biannual "staff development assembly" in Boston, so that meant an extra week off for the students. For me, that meant two entire weeks of participating in an intensive, invitation-only riding clinic on campus. And two weeks to make Callie understand that Eric and I were *just friends*.

At the end of the Junior Equestrian Regionals, Mr. Conner, my tough but kindhearted riding instructor, had invited Julia Myer, Alison Robb, Heather Fox, Callie Harper, and me to participate. Three instructors from other top New England schools had signed up to teach classes. Fifteen other students and horses were arriving this weekend to settle in for the start of the clinic on Monday.

When Callie and I first found out about the clinic, we'd been so excited about spending two whole weeks together. We'd been instant best friends since I'd enrolled at Canterwood a year ago September. During all of those months, Callie had never been interested in guys—until Eric. Even though she'd never asked him out, Callie'd had a crush on Eric since he started at Canterwood in January.

Paige had left to say goodbye to some friends from cooking class before she went home for break tomorrow morning. Mr. and Mrs. Parker were picking her up so she could stay at home in Manhattan while she spent two weeks filming episodes for *Teen Cuisine*. I half wanted to go with her, to get away from the anti-Sasha people on campus.

I checked my watch. Sitting in my room wasn't fun and my horse, Charm, was probably just as bored alone in his stall. But the meeting with Mr. Conner and the rest of the advanced team wasn't for a few hours.

Ugh. And Callie, who was part of that team, would be there and probably ignoring me again. A pang of sadness went through me. This clinic was supposed to be the highlight of our semester. Maybe she'd magically start to believe me and we'd stop fighting. Riiight.

I pulled on a black riding boot. What if Callie saw me at the meeting and just walked away again? I shook my head. I still couldn't believe the way she'd been acting. I'd said a *zillion* times that Eric and I weren't flirting or whatever she thought we were doing. I wished she would just believe me that I still liked Jacob. But who knew, maybe I wouldn't even see Callie. Today was check-in day for Mr. Conner's clinic, and the stable would be filled with new riders.

I tugged on my other boot, deciding that now was *not* the time to obsess about Callie or Jacob. Charm and I had to focus and get ready for the clinic Monday. So that's what we would do. When I stood to leave, I saw Eric's black coat hanging on the back of my desk chair. Oops—I

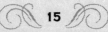

needed to return that. I picked it up and Eric's scent washed over me—like clean laundry and mint. I folded the coat and dropped it into a Macy's bag, smiling at the comfort it brought me.

When I got to the stable, I peered around the corner. No sign of Callie. Phew! As I strolled down the aisle, I walked by Luna's stall and saw that the flea-bitten gray mare wasn't inside. I looked around and finally saw Eric and Luna, the stable horse he borrowed for lessons, at the far end of the aisle. He had the mare in crossties and it looked like he was trying to thin her mane.

"Need some help?" I called, putting the bag on the counter.

Eric almost dropped the pulling comb. "Is it that obvious? I'm horrible at this. Poor Luna." He patted her neck. "I know she can't feel it, but *I* feel bad that I'm doing such an awful job."

I laughed, eyeing Luna's mane—it was thick near her poll and thinner by her withers. "Well . . . you did a good job on the middle!"

Eric laughed. "So, equine expert, what should I do?"

"I'll show you. Oh, that's your coat in the bag on the counter, by the way. Sorry I forgot to give it back before."

"No problem," Eric said.

He handed me the silver comb and I grabbed an empty water bucket from the stall next to us. I stepped up to Luna's shoulder and patted her. She snorted, probably relieved that Eric was getting help, and stood still. I turned the bucket upside down and stood on it, holding onto Luna's neck to steady myself.

I looked down at Eric. "You want to grab a small bit of mane with your left hand and with your right . . . ," I demonstrated with the comb. "Pull the comb upward fast. Do that a few times and you'll have the longer hairs left in your hand."

Eric looked at the way my hand clutched the mane. "Okay. I can see that."

"Now, wrap those long strands around the comb and pull down hard. But do it fast so you don't tug on her neck for too long."

Eric watched as I pulled a few more sections. "Wow, you're good at that."

"It just takes practice. Here, you try."

Eric took the comb, grabbed a chunk of Luna's mane and tried to pull upward. The hunk of mane turned into a snarl around the comb.

"Eric!" I said, smothering a laugh.

He ran his fingers through his thick, dark hair. "It's

not supposed to do that!" He tried to untangle the comb, but Luna's coarse mane knotted around the teeth.

"Oh, man," I said. "You're making it worse!" I laughed out loud this time and climbed back onto the bucket, gently pushing Eric out of the way.

I concentrated on Luna's tangled mess and took my time pulling the strands of mane from around the comb.

"Almost . . . got . . . it," I said. After a couple more tugs, the final pieces of mane came loose. "There!" I turned to grin at Eric, but as I did, the bucket wobbled. I went to grab for Luna's mane, but the bucket tilted too fast and threw me off balance. "Ahhh!"

Eric jumped in front of me to catch me before I ended up in a heap on the aisle floor. I smacked against his chest and he let out an *oof* as we both staggered backward a couple of steps. Eric kept us upright—keeping us both from falling onto the concrete floor.

"You okay?" he asked. A blush crept up my neck.

"I'm so sorry!" I blurted out.

"Hey, it was worth almost getting pulverized to have your help with Luna's mane."

"*Excuse* me?" My eyebrows shot up. "Pulverized? Are you saying I'm HEAVY?" I tried to look serious, but I couldn't hide my smile.

He laughed. "Of course not! I'm just saying—" He stopped in midsentence and stared over my shoulder.

"What?"

Eric let me go. It didn't even register until just then that our faces had been inches apart and he'd still been holding my arms. When I turned to follow his nervous glance, I wasn't surprised to see Callie standing there. *Great,* I thought, hoping she'd at least seen the part where I'd fallen off the bucket.

But Callie only glared at me before spinning on her boot heel and heading back down the aisle.

Oookay. Guess not.

"Callie!" I jogged after her. "Wait!"

I grabbed her arm and she stopped, yanking it out of my grasp. "What?" she spat.

"Please," I said. "Can we just talk?"

"You don't need to talk to *me*."

"Why not? You're my best friend!"

Callie laughed. "I used to be. But why so worried? You've got *Eric* now."

"No, I don't!" I lowered my voice so the entire stable couldn't hear me. "Eric and I are friends, Callie. I swear. Why won't you believe me?"

Callie took a breath. "Oh, I don't know, Sasha. It's kind

19

of hard to believe you when you were just close enough to kiss the guy."

She stared at me for another second before stomping into the bathroom and slamming the door behind her. The lock clicked.

I rubbed my forehead with my hand. If only Callie would let me explain what had just happened with Eric. I leaned against the wall, waiting for Callie to come out. Minutes ticked by and she didn't emerge. I sighed, turning away from the door, and slowly walked away.

Riding didn't sound like so much fun after any of this, but Charm needed the exercise. And, I reminded myself, it was better than sulking alone in my room. I grabbed his gear from the tack room and shuffled past Eric and Luna.

"You okay?" he asked.

"Fine," I grumbled. "Sorry, Eric—you didn't do anything wrong. I just need to be alone for a little while."

Eric looked as if he wanted to say something, but he just nodded and went back to Luna's mane. Reluctantly, I walked away from him.

3

GUESS WHO'S COMING TO CANTERWOOD?

"HI, BOY," I SAID TO CHARM. HE PRICKED HIS ears at my voice and came up to the stall door. I set his tack on the counter and led him out to an empty pair of crossties. His glossy chestnut coat shined from his daily groomings. All he needed was a quick run over with a body brush to flick off the hay stalks that clung to his sides.

"We have to hurry so we don't see Callie again," I whispered to him. Charm turned his head as far as the crossties would allow to look at me. I whisked the brush over his body with record speed and plopped the saddle pad onto his back.

Charm snorted and stepped sideways.

"Charm," I snapped, surprised. "Stop it."

I gathered the English saddle in my arms and put it on

his back. Charm's ears went back as I tightened the girth and pulled down the stirrups. When I slipped the reins over his head and took off his halter, he turned his head away from me and looked down the aisle.

I guided his head back toward me and held the bit on my palm. Charm raised his muzzle away from my hand and clenched his teeth shut.

"Charm!" He'd *never* not taken the bit. I put my hand under his muzzle again, but he tossed his head and stamped his front left hoof. "Fine." I stuck my index finger in the corner of his mouth and pressed down. Charm opened his mouth from the pressure and I slipped the bit inside. "Let's go," I grumbled to him. I put on my helmet as we walked down the aisle.

We were just feet away from Callie's horse, Black Jack. I glanced around, but didn't see her. We had almost passed Jack's stall, when Charm dug his heels into the aisle and stopped.

"Charm, c'mon!" I tugged on the reins, something I would have done my first week as a rider. Charm strained his head toward Jack's stall.

"Charm!" I stepped back by his shoulder and tried to lead him forward again. His ears went back and he glanced in Jack's direction again before finally deciding to follow me.

When we reached the grassy yard, I turned to look at him. "I'm doing you a favor! I didn't want to come to the stable today, but I thought *you* wanted to get out of your stall. What's your problem?" I looked around to be sure no one saw crazy Sasha arguing with her horse. The arena and yards were empty.

The weak sun struggled to peek out from behind thick gray clouds and shadows that covered some of the mostly empty campus. The sidewalks that snaked through the raked lawn were deserted. A black four-horse trailer rumbled down the driveway—someone had probably arrived for clinic check-in.

I put Charm's reins in my left hand and aimed my foot at the stirrup iron. At the last minute, Charm shifted sideways and my foot missed. I lifted my leg again and got my toe in the iron, but Charm started to walk forward.

"Hey, whoa!" I said. I tugged on the reins and hopped along on one foot. Charm snorted and stopped. I bounced on my right foot and got into the saddle before he started moving again. "Bad manners, boy. You know better."

I dismounted and made Charm stand still while I mounted again. I tapped my heels against his sides and he broke into a trot, tossing his head against the reins and jerking them through my fingers. It took almost ten

minutes to get him from the stable to the arena and my arms shook from trying to keep his head up. I wanted to get off and take him back to the stable, but I couldn't end the lesson on such a bad note.

Charm fought my hands and legs as I angled him along the arena fence and worked to keep him at a trot. He bounced forward, increasing his speed.

"Trot," I said. "Not canter. Trot."

Charm kept both ears forward, not listening to my voice. What if Mr. Conner saw this? He'd selected me for the advanced clinic and I was having problems before it even started!

"Charm, please. You're eight—not three." I halted him and dismounted *again*. "Is something wrong with your tack?"

I loosened his girth and ran my hands under the saddle pad, checking for a wrinkle or something that could irritate him. After his pad checked out, I looked at the corners of his mouth to be sure the bridle wasn't too tight.

"Nothing's wrong with your tack, and you're not acting sick," I said, mounting. "Let's get to work, okay? Maybe you just need exercise."

Charm moved quickly into a trot, then a choppy, uneven canter. Sitting to the bumpy gait wasn't easy. We made it halfway around the arena and his stride started to even out.

"Good boy. That's more like—" But before I could finish my sentence, Charm dipped his head and launched his hindquarters into the air.

He bucked hard and I wasn't prepared enough to sit through it. My feet popped out of the stirrups. I grabbed for Charm's mane but missed and flew over his shoulder. I soared through the air and—WHAM—landed on my back on the hard arena dirt.

I gasped and sucked in cold air as I looked up at the gray sky. I flexed my arms and legs; nothing felt broken. But I wanted to disappear into the dirt. What had gotten into him?

Two sets of hoofbeats pounded the arena dirt. I sat up and watched Heather catch Charm and lead him over to me. She dismounted from Aristocrat, her Thoroughbred gelding, and held both horses' reins.

Great, I thought. Flashes of my first day at Canterwood hit me. Charm had spooked, bolted, and caused Heather to fall. Now, I was on the ground and Heather was the LAST person I wanted to see after everything she'd done to mess up my relationship with Jacob.

"You okay?" Heather asked.

She crouched beside my shoulder and scanned me with her clear blue eyes.

"Fine," I grumbled. "Just got the wind knocked out of me."

Heather stood and reached a caramel-colored, cashmere-gloved hand out to me. "That was a tough buck," she said. "What's wrong with Charm?"

I ignored her hand and stood on my own. "I don't know. I'll figure it out."

I took Charm's reins from her and watched as she mounted Aristocrat. Her golden blond hair popped against the apple-red peacoat she wore, and I thought for the millionth time how unfair it was that someone so mean could also be so beautiful.

Her dark chestnut horse looked away from Charm and struck the dirt with his foreleg. I turned away from Heather and Aristocrat and started to lead Charm toward the stable. I'd had enough humiliation for one day—I just wanted to go back to my room.

"What are you doing?" Heather asked.

I didn't look back. "Not that it's any of your business, but I'm taking him back to the stable."

Heather angled Aristocrat in front of the gate, blocking our way. "You're *not* going back."

I couldn't believe it! What was this girl's problem? "Why do you care what I do? You should be *happy*. Jacob hates me, my best friend won't talk to me—even my horse doesn't seem to like me today."

"Sasha, get real. If you and Jacob were so cozy, you wouldn't have believed that he kissed me in the first place. You would have just trusted him." She shrugged. "Sad that you didn't just do what you normally do so well—not listen to me."

I glared up at her. "But why did you even do it? You were with *Ben* five minutes later! Are you dating him for real or just messing with Julia, too?"

Heather shook her head. She dropped the knotted reins on Aristocrat's neck and crossed her arms. "Like I'd tell *you* that."

I pulled Charm a few feet forward and his ears inched back as we got closer to Aristocrat. "Forget it. I really don't care."

Heather didn't let Aristocrat move. "I'm not letting you through."

I groaned and fought the urge to scream. I didn't want to be anywhere near her. "Move, Heather. Just let me go back to the stable."

"No. I don't care about the stupid Soirée and I don't

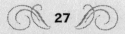

27

want to hear you whine about Jacob. *You* are part of Canterwood's advanced team and as much as I'd looove for you to fail, you can't. You have to ride well or it reflects badly on all of us—Callie, Julia, Alison, and me. So, shut up and get on your horse."

I huffed. "You're kidding me."

"I'm going to pony you on Charm if you don't get on right now."

"Oh, God." The last thing I needed was for Mr. Conner to see Heather leading me on Charm.

I jammed my foot into the stirrup and lifted myself into Charm's saddle, furious. He was quiet now—apologetic that he'd tossed me.

I fake-grinned and looked at Heather. "Happy?"

"Not till I see you ride."

I turned Charm back toward the arena's center hating every moment of this. Heather kept an eye on me and moved Aristocrat away from the exit. Charm's ears flicked back for cues and I let him move into a trot. He was on his best behavior now that Aristocrat, his number one rival, watched him. Heather let Aristocrat match Charm's stride, but I refused to look at her as we lapped the arena.

Her words about trust nagged at me. What if she was right? Maybe my relationship with Jacob had crumbled

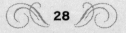

because I didn't trust him. If Jacob and I had been as close as I'd thought we were, none of this would have happened. We would have talked about Heather and I wouldn't have been so paranoid.

After half an hour of riding with Heather, she finally let me go. We cooled our horses and headed to the skybox for our riding team meeting.

The stable was busier now that people were arriving to check in for the clinic. I passed a window that overlooked the parking lot. Half a dozen trailers filled the lot. Students circled horses and Mike and Doug, my two favorite grooms, pointed in the direction of the stable. I looked away from the window and walked to the skybox.

Inside the room, Callie, sitting between Julia and Alison, texted on her BlackBerry without even glancing in my direction.

"Well, well, look who came in together," Alison said, lookng back and forth between me and Heather. She brushed a lock of her sandy brown hair out of her eye. "You two losers deserve each other."

"What does *that* mean?" I said, looking at Heather. Did they *all* think I'd stolen Eric from Callie?

"Good, you're all here!" Mr. Conner boomed, walking into the room.

Heather and I slid into our seats, far away from Julia, Alison, and Callie. Mr. Conner stood at the front of the room and paged through a white plastic binder.

"Let's get right to business," he said. "The clinic is a wonderful opportunity for you to learn and grow as riders. Fifteen other top equestrian students will be coming from nearby schools to participate. And, at the end of the clinic, there will be a demonstration to show off your new skills."

"So, it's a show?" Heather asked. I could practically see the blue ribbons flashing in her eyes.

"No, there won't be ribbons or rankings," Mr. Conner said. "It's more of a chance for you to prove to scouts from the Youth Equestrian National Team that you're serious candidates for the eighth-grade team."

My heart pounded faster when he said *scouts*. Charm and I would have to practice our hardest to impress them. We *had* to make the YENT. The YENT, a Junior Olympic–like team, would put us on track to one day ride on the United States Equestrian Team.

"Full details about the clinic will be explained to the entire group of riders on Monday morning. So, please enjoy your day off tomorrow—"

Beep!

A text alert cut Mr. Conner off and everyone turned to

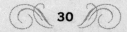

see whose phone went off. Callie, leaning down, scrambled to find her phone in her bag.

"I'm so sorry, Mr. Conner," Callie said. "I guess I forgot to turn it—" But the look on Mr. Conner's face stopped her midsentence. His dark eyes zeroed in on her and made the rest of us so nervous that we surreptitiously checked to make sure our own phones were turned off too.

"Ms. Harper, do we all need to stay and go through this stable's cell phone policy?" Mr. Conner asked.

"No," Callie whispered.

"This will *not* happen while scouts and visiting instructors are present. If a phone from a Canterwood rider goes off during a meeting or class, she's out for the day. Understand?"

We nodded and Callie ducked her head. Last week, I would have tried to shift Mr. Conner's annoyance away from Callie. But now, she was on her own. If she was going to spread lies and join forces with Julia and Alison—if they were going to be the new evil Trio—that was her choice, not mine.

"You may all go now." Mr. Conner dismissed us with a wave of his hand. Callie hurried out the door and Heather and I let Julia and Alison go after her before we left the room.

The main aisle was crowded with riders and strange horses. I already missed the quiet of the stable before sure-to-be-awesome riders had invaded it.

Two stalls down, a steel gray horse's head poked over the stall door. Where had I seen him? He looked so familiar. . . .

Oh.

My.

God.

It was Phoenix.

"If it isn't Sasha Silver from *Union!*" Jasmine King peeked out of Phoenix's stall door and grinned at me.

I groaned. Jasmine, a rider for Wellington Prep, had been Canterwood's nastiest rival at the Junior Equestrian Regionals, a big show a couple of weeks ago in Fairfield. She'd gone out of her way to remind me that I didn't belong on *her* show circuit.

Jasmine closed the door behind her and stepped in front of me. Her dark chocolate brown hair had been curled into soft waves and her peach-colored lips glowed shiny and bright against her fair skin.

"You're here for the clinic," I grumbled.

"Aw, Sasha! Don't say it like that! We're going to have a *fabulous* two weeks together." Jas's eyes brightened as she

spoke, but I knew better. She was going to try to make me and my teammates miserable!

"Whatever. I've got to go," I said. I walked past her, trying not to choke on the cloud of vanilla body spray that surrounded her.

"Wait a sec."

I stopped and turned back. "What?"

Jasmine's tall boots clicked down the aisle as she walked over to me. She stuck out her arm and brushed at some dirt on my right shoulder.

"The clinic hasn't even started yet and you've already taken a spill?" Jasmine asked. She folded her arms. "You should just go home to Mommy and Daddy now. You can't compete with us."

I laughed and Jasmine took a half step back. "That's *so* funny!" I said. "'Cause if I remember regionals, and I think I do, I beat *you*." I smiled and gave a little wave. "See ya."

Without a backward glance, I took my time walking out of the stable. I felt Jasmine's eyes on my back. I'd beaten her today, but I knew it wasn't over. I'd only just raised the stakes.

Later that night, I was back at Winchester trying to figure out how to ask Paige to FedEx me homemade food from NYC.

"Maybe I shouldn't leave," Paige said. "Callie is ignoring you, Heather's being weirdly friendly, and Jasmine's going to be in your face for two whole weeks!"

I twirled on the swivel stool in Winchester's common room kitchen. Paige was making kettle corn on the stovetop and the salty-sweet smell made my mouth water. "You have to go—it's *Teen Cuisine!*"

Paige smiled. "But you know I'd stay if you needed me."

"I'll be fine." I had to get a grip. Paige should have been happy about her dream gig at *TC*, but instead she was worried about me. "You're a good friend, but you're crazy. I'm going to be okay."

"Just promise me you'll focus on riding," Paige said. "Forget about Jasmine and Heather. Work on getting your friendship back with Callie, but don't push her. She'll talk to you when she's ready."

"If she's *ever* ready. I don't know why she won't believe me about Eric."

"She will . . . eventually," Paige said. "You're her best friend. She'll realize that." Paige tossed a piece of kettle corn at me and I smiled.

"I'll starve while you're gone," I teased, clutching my stomach.

Paige rolled her eyes and sighed. "Sadly, I believe you."

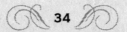

4

TRAIL RIDE = TROUBLE

DAYS TILL CLINIC: 1
DAYS SINCE CALLIE HAS STOPPED BEING MY BFF: 3

SUNDAY TV WAS THE WORST. PAIGE HAD LEFT for NYC two hours ago and I'd been flipping through channels and trying to distract myself. Nothing worked. Not even Animal Planet.

Even Eric was probably home by now. I wished, once again, that he was on the advanced team. With Eric around, I wouldn't feel so alone.

I considered my options. I could go groom Charm, but then I'd probably run into someone I didn't want to see. And what if Charm was still being bratty? I couldn't handle that today.

I flopped onto my stomach on my bed and sighed.

When my phone started buzzing on the table, I flipped it open. Eric Rodriguez flashed on the screen.

"Hi," I said. "Glad to be home for break?"

"Well," Eric said. "I *was* going to go home, but something else came up."

I flicked off the TV. "Like what?"

"I got an offer to assist a riding instructor during break. He thinks I have potential and if I help out, I'll get to learn a ton."

"Eric! That's great! What stable?"

He laughed. "Canterwood. Mr. Conner asked me."

I smiled into the phone. "You're staying for break? Really?" Finally! Something was going right! I already felt less lonely knowing that Eric would be around.

"Really. So why don't you come trail ride with me and you can tell me more about the clinic."

I paused. "I don't know. Charm's been kind of a pain lately and—"

"Maybe he needs a break from lessons. C'mon, it'll be fun."

Honestly, it *did* sound fun. The only reason I didn't say yes right away had nothing to do with Charm, either. The truth was, I was afraid of what Callie would say. But thanks to Callie, I didn't have any other friends on campus as the moment, so why was I so worried about what *she* would think?

"Okay," I said. "You're probably right. Meet you in twenty minutes?"

"See you then," Eric said.

I pushed end and looked at my phone. The wallpaper was a picture of Jacob that Callie had snapped a few days ago. I scrolled under "options" and changed my wallpaper to a picture of Charm. A trail ride sounded so much better than being alone and missing my friends.

When I got to the stable, Eric had Luna crosstied and Charm's tack was on the counter.

"Hey, thanks," I said.

"No prob. Faster we tack up the more time we have to ride."

Charm was quiet while I groomed him and got him ready. I kept glancing around for Callie or Jasmine, but neither showed up. Eric and I buckled on our helmets and led the horses outside.

As we hopped into our saddles, I noticed how comfortable Eric looked on Luna. His boots were tucked into his black breeches and he had on a well-worn hunter green pullover.

"Where to?" I asked.

Eric half stood in the stirrups and pointed to the woods behind Blackwell, one of the guys' dorms. "How about that way?"

"Let's go!"

The forty-something-degree air made my cheeks tingle and I adjusted the purple scarf around my neck. I dug into my pocket and pulled out my Red Raspberry Lip Smackers. As I smoothed it on, I looked around at the quiet campus. The wooden benches, usually crowded with students, were empty. Even the steps outside the library were desolate. Most of the buildings—usually ablaze with lights—were dark.

Charm moved into an even walk and matched his stride to Luna's. The mare eyed Charm and the horses sniffed muzzles.

"I think Charm likes her," Eric said.

"Poor guy. The only mare he gets to hang out with during lessons is Julia's mare Trix. He gets along with her about as well as I do with Julia."

We laughed. Soon, the campus was behind us and we found a dirt path that led into the woods. The trail was wide enough for us to walk our horses side by side, so I pulled Charm beside Luna.

"So, tell me," I said. "How'd you get the gig as Mr. Conner's assistant?"

Eric shifted in the saddle to look at me. "Mr. Conner called me into his office about a week ago. He said he was going to be busy with the clinic and he needed someone to help him keep track of the new riders and instructors. He said if I'd help, he'd let me sit in and watch a few lessons."

"Wow, that's great experience."

Eric nodded. "I know. Mr. Conner said he thought I'd learn a lot and it would help me when I test for the advanced team in the fall."

"Definitely! And, hello—I can't believe you didn't tell me about this before now."

Eric looked at Luna's mane and then back at me. "You had a lot going on with . . . things."

I was quiet for a minute.

"Yeah," I finally said. "But I've got to focus on the clinic and riding in general. This is a huge chance to prove to the scouts that I should be on the YENT. Plus, you're my friend. I always have time to listen to stuff going on in *your* life."

Eric guided Luna closer. "You'll show those scouts."

We smiled at each other. Eric always made me feel comfortable, like we'd known each other forever.

I watched him on Luna—he was a skilled rider. He didn't overpower Luna with hard hands or forceful legs. He listened to her. Luna and Charm, exhilarated by the brisk air, shook out their manes and tugged at the reins.

"Do you want to trot?" I asked.

Without answering, Eric let Luna take off.

"Hey!" I called. Charm trotted after them and I laughed as he edged his nose in front of Luna's. Then Luna inched in front of Charm. I let Charm out a notch and he was in front again.

We weaved the horses through the woods and edged them around full evergreens and barren oak trees. Their hooves pounded the hard dirt and their hoofbeats seemed to resound through the quiet woods. Two cardinals, a bright red male and a brown female, scolded angrily as they flew up from a low-hanging tree branch.

Eric and I made faces at each other and let our horses battle for the lead.

After our ride, we cooled and groomed the horses. I latched Charm's stall shut while Eric waited for me.

"That was fun," I said. "I really needed it."

"And Charm didn't seem to have any problems," Eric added, leaning against the stall next to Charm's.

"Nope. It was my fault the other day. I probably stressed him out."

I peered in at Charm, who had already stuffed his face with hay. Stalks stuck out of his mouth and he had droplets of water dribbling down his chin.

I laughed and absently rubbed my hands up and down the arms of my thin yellow sweater.

"Cold?" Eric asked.

"Freezing," I said.

"It was pretty cold on the ride. Want to get something hot to drink from the Sweet Shoppe?"

I looked at him. Could I do that? Even though I knew it wasn't a date, Eric was still a guy. *But he's just a friend,* I reminded myself. *The only reason you're even hesitating is because of Callie.*

"Um . . . ," I said, brilliantly.

"They have a new mint hot chocolate and their apple cider is awesome," he said.

Charm snorted and bobbed his head.

"What, boy?" I asked. "Apple?"

Charm's upper lip flapped up and down. Eric and I laughed until our stomachs were sore.

"I guess that's a sign," I said.

"Do you mind if I stop by Winchester and change

first?" I asked, as we walked out of the stable. "Last week, I got the death stare when I came in covered in horse hair."

"Good idea. I'll walk you to Winchester, go back to my dorm to change, and then swing back to Winchester to meet you."

"Perfect," I said.

The grounds were deserted. We walked past the courtyard where we'd seen Heather and Ben on Valentine's Day. I shoved the memory out of my brain. We were almost to Winchester when I spotted someone pacing around outside the entrance.

"Is that . . . ?" I said.

Callie! Maybe she'd come over to let me explain! But she turned and her smile disappeared the instant she saw Eric beside me. Before I could say anything, she bolted down the steps.

"Callie, wait!" I left Eric standing there and went after her.

Callie stopped and her nostrils flared. "What?"

"I-I—" I wasn't sure what to say with Eric nearby. I couldn't embarrass Callie by saying anything about the fact that Callie had a crush on him.

"I want to talk," I tried again. "Can I come over later? Please?"

Callie hesitated.

"Callie, please. You're my best friend. I miss you. Things just got mixed up—I promise it's not at all what you think."

Callie looked at Eric over my shoulder. She pulled the collar of her snow-white wool coat up to her chin, and fidgeted with a button on the sleeve.

"Maybe," she said.

I beamed. "Really?"

"If you want, to, later," Callie said. "We can go trail riding and talk as we ride?"

"Did you say 'trail riding'?" Eric asked. "Because Sasha and I just found the coolest trail." He gave me a look as if he thought he was helping. "You guys should totally go on that one. Sasha, if you want, we can meet up later. I don't mind."

I wanted to clap my hand over his mouth, but it was too late.

Callie stepped back, the all-too-familiar frown clouding her face once again. "Never mind. I've gotta go."

"Cal, no!" I cried. But this time she didn't turn around.

Eric looked at me and knitted his eyebrows with concern. "What happened? Did I say something wrong?"

I felt bad for him—he had no idea what was going on and I really couldn't tell him. "No, she's upset about something else. I'll talk to her later."

"Oh . . . well, okay. We can talk about it at the Sweet Shoppe—figure out how to fix things, maybe? I'll be back in twenty minutes to pick you up," Eric said.

I shoved my hands in my coat pockets. "Eric, I want to go, but I can't. I'm sorry. I just need to figure out things with Callie on my own."

Eric didn't argue. "Understood. Well, maybe after our next ride."

"Deal."

He smiled at me before walking away. I'd thought I was making the right decision, but with every step farther away that Eric got, I wondered. I hadn't done anything wrong, and Callie seemed determined to hate me anyway.

I thought about how great Eric had been since everything had blown up at the Soirée. Was it worth giving up a really good friend for someone who seemed angry at me no matter *what* I did?

5

AND SO IT BEGINS

RIDING CLINIC ORIENTATION DAY. GULP. I peered into the stable's meeting room. It was packed. Usually, I only met with my seventh-grade advanced team-mates, but now there were fifteen other students in the room.

Callie, flanked by Julia and Alison, sat in the center of the room. Callie looked chic in a new light blue and white—striped v-neck sweater and beige breeches. If we were still friends, we would be talking about exactly where she got the sweater, if those colors would look good on me, and when we could go shopping so I could get one too.

I grabbed a chair off to the side and looked behind me

at Callie. But she didn't even glance up from her phone. Texting. Again. I wondered who she was even texting—she never used to text when we'd hung out!

Behind Callie, Julia, and Alison, Jasmine sat with pink earbuds in her ears. I turned back around when she caught me looking at her.

Heather, looking polished and pretty in white breeches, a hunter green and gold argyle long-sleeve shirt and expensive-looking brown leather boots, walked into the room and took the seat next to me.

"Why are you sitting next to *me*?" I whispered.

Heather rolled her eyes and leaned closer. "Because sitting next to you is only somewhat less pathetic than sitting by myself."

I knew I shouldn't have asked.

Mr. Conner stepped into the room and three people— one man and two women—followed him.

"Welcome, everyone! I'm Mr. Conner, the instructor at Canterwood Crest. Thank you all for coming to our riding clinic. Before we begin, allow me to introduce my colleagues."

I craned my neck to see and Heather did the same.

"Your jumping coach will be Virginia Thorne from St. Anne's Preparatory in Vermont. Ms. Thorne has trained

riders for the United States Equestrian Team and she's a former Grand Prix competitor."

Ms. Thorne stepped forward and nodded at us. There was no trace of a smile on her face. She was insanely tall and supermodel skinny. But she was more gangly than modellike.

"Your flatwork and dressage instructor is Miss Abby Cho," Mr. Conner said. "She has been teaching students for fifteen years and many of her riders have gone on to win national competitions."

Miss Cho waved at us and smiled. She was petite and had straight black hair, which she wore in a low ponytail. She looked especially tiny next to Ms. Thorne.

"And finally," Mr. Conner said. "You'll learn about horse nutrition, holistic remedies and relaxation techniques from Mr. Edwin Bright. Mr. Bright has worked with some of the country's best horse whisperers including Monty Roberts and Pat Parelli. You're all fortunate to have the opportunity work with him."

"*The Horse Whisperer* is one of my favorite movies," I whispered to Heather.

Mr. Bright dipped his head to us. His gray hair was cropped short and he was tan—probably from spending hours taming wild horses on a ranch.

I looked at the four adults standing in front of us. I was sure they'd have different teaching styles—I'd have to adapt to the different styles. But most of the students here were probably like Callie—they'd already worked with different instructors from some of the best riding schools. What if I was the only one who hadn't?

"We're going to break you up into groups of five," Miss Cho said. "Ms. Thorne and I will briefly evaluate your skills." Miss Cho took a clipboard off the table. "All right. Group A. Julia Myer, Alison Robb, Kristin Henderson, Georgia Walker, and Callie Harper."

I looked behind me as Callie, Julia, and Alison high-fived and giggled together.

Ms. Thorne called out Group B, which included Heather and four other girls.

"Group C," Miss Cho said. "Will be Jasmine King, Violet Locke, Cole Martin, Sasha Silver, and Aaron Thompson."

Great—Jasmine. I didn't know Aaron or Cole, but Violet was from Canterwood. She was on the eighth-grade advanced team.

Miss Cho assigned the rest of the groups and Ms. Thorne stepped forward.

"Get your horses tacked and be in the indoor arena in

twenty minutes," she said in a deep voice. "Or you'll be watching the lesson from the ground."

Heather and I both stood up.

"I'm *so* glad you're in my group, Sash!" Jasmine said. She smiled and then looked at Heather. "Have you been avoiding me? I haven't seen you since I got here!"

Heather crossed her arms. "Please. Like I have any reason to avoid *you*. But if you even *think* about getting in my face, I'll send you right back to Wellington."

Jasmine's smile slipped.

I left for the tack room, with Heather on my heels, and kept an eye on my watch the entire time. This was going to be an interesting day.

6

GROUP C, F RIDE

"LISTEN UP!" MS. THORNE SAID TO MY GROUP.
Violet, Cole, Jasmine, Aaron, and I had our horses lined
up in front of her. "You are Group C. Remember the
people in your group. You'll be riding and learning with
them for the next two weeks. Today, Miss Cho and I will
be rotating among the groups."

I wondered what Callie, Julia, and Alison were doing
in their group.

"But we're wasting time talking. Let's get to work."
Ms. Thorne folded her arms and moved to the center of
the arena.

I took a deep breath. Charm eyed the other horses
around us.

"Warm up with two laps at a walk and then do the same at a trot."

The five of us moved our horses along the wall. Violet urged her bay gelding in front of Charm and used her hands to encourage her horse to stretch. She rode as if she'd already graduated from the clinic.

Aaron, who had rich, mocha-colored skin just a shade lighter than Callie's and dark hair that was buzzed close to his scalp, led in front. His seat was as quiet as Violet's. I swallowed. Charm and I had to be the least trained pair here.

Ms. Thorne put up a hand after we'd made four circuits around the arena. "Canter, please," she said. She left the arena's center and walked over to a folding table along the wall where she had a stack of folders.

I let Charm move into a canter just behind Violet's horse. Charm flicked an ear back as hoofbeats pounded too close behind us.

I looked over my shoulder. Jasmine and Phoenix rode up on Charm's heels. She'd let him edge up so close behind us that his muzzle almost bumped Charm's tail!

Charm snorted and tossed his head. He couldn't go any faster, or we'd crowd Violet's horse. Jasmine was *not* forcing

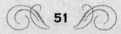

me out of line. I waited for Ms. Thorne to say something, but she was still shuffling through the folders.

"Jasmine!" I hissed. "Back off!"

But she only let Phoenix inch closer. Charm *hated* it when horses tailgated. He put back his ears and his canter changed from smooth to choppy.

"Ms. King and Ms. Silver!" Ms. Thorne snapped. "Either space your horses properly or leave my class."

Jasmine checked Phoenix and he dropped back three strides. I couldn't believe Ms. Thorne had yelled at me! Charm and I hadn't done anything. If Callie were here, she'd . . . no. I reminded myself to focus.

A few more laps and the horses were warmed up. Mike and Doug came into the arena and set up three verticals of increasing heights to just over three feet.

"Ms. Locke, you'll ride first. Begin when you're ready."

Violet turned her horse in a slow circle before pointing him at the first red and white vertical. Her horse tucked his knees and lifted into the air. Violet barely moved in the saddle—her technique was flawless. Her style reminded me of Heather's. She piloted her horse over the course. She took the other jumps in the same style and rejoined our group. Ms. Thorne gave her a nod and marked off something on her clipboard.

"Ms. King," Ms. Thorne said. "Your turn."

Jasmine couldn't have been more different than Violet. She kicked Phoenix forward without giving him a circle or two to settle. She lifted early in the saddle and signaled for Phoenix to leave the ground too soon. Just to show off, Jasmine forced him to work harder and jump higher than he needed to.

Jasmine urged him forward with her hands, almost shoving them along his neck, and made him do a fast canter in the short space to the second jump. Phoenix cleared it, but the gray gelding wasn't relaxed as Violet's horse had been. Phoenix took the last jump and Jasmine rode him toward us.

"Someone tell me why that was a ride I never want to see again in my class," Ms. Thorne said.

Cole, a cute, lanky guy with light brown hair, raised his hand. Jasmine glared at him. He saw her gaze and slowly lowered his arm. But Ms. Thorne had already seen his hand.

"Mr. Martin?" Ms. Thorne asked.

Cole's eyes shifted to Jasmine before he cleared his throat. "She, uh, rode with too much force. She pushed her horse over every jump. He would have been exhausted if the course had been a normal length."

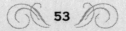

Jasmine sat up straighter in her saddle. "I did *not* force Phoenix over the jumps," she said. "He doesn't listen if I just sit there."

"But you don't have to handle him roughly," Ms. Thorne said. "Next time, I want to see softer hands and legs. You're a good enough rider not to be quite so forceful, correct?"

"Yes," Jasmine said. Her cheeks blushed to match her raspberry lip gloss.

"All right, let's get back to riding," Ms. Thorne said. "Ms. Silver, it's your turn."

I let Charm into a trot and circled him. My mind should have been on the jumps, but I couldn't focus with Jasmine glaring at me. I just wished I had at least *one* friend in my group.

I pointed Charm at the first vertical. *What was Callie doing in her class?* I wondered as I signaled Charm to take off. He rose into the air a half-stride too late and clipped the rail.

Pay attention! I screamed at myself silently. I glued my eyes to the next jump and focused on getting Charm over it. He huffed and shook his mane as we cantered to the last blue and white vertical. This time, he gathered his hindquarters under him and bounded over the jump— way too high—as Phoenix had done.

I eased him to a trot and got back into line.

What a disaster!

"It would have been a cleaner ride, Ms. Silver, if you had paid attention," Ms. Thorne said. She scribbled something on my chart.

I nodded, wishing Charm and I could slip out the door and never come back. But the clinic had just started and there was a long, long way to go.

"I've taken notes on areas for improvement," Ms. Thorne said, minutes later. "Tomorrow, we'll begin to work. I suggest you get to bed early tonight."

I shifted in the saddle.

"Please walk your horses until Miss Cho arrives for your flatwork and dressage lesson," she said. Ms. Thorne tipped her head to us and left the arena.

Charm hadn't walked two steps before Violet angled her horse beside me. Even though she was in eighth grade, her gray eyeliner, rosy lip gloss, and expertly braided chocolate brown hair made her look much older than her classmates.

"What's his name?" she asked me.

"Charm," I said. "Yours?"

"Hunter. You're on the seventh-grade advanced team, right?" Violet asked.

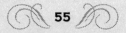

"Yeah, I made it last fall."

As we talked, I noticed Jasmine slow Phoenix and try to eavesdrop on our conversation. I let Charm out half a stride.

"I've seen you ride before," Violet said, lowering her voice. "Are you having an off day?"

"I know, it's so embarrassing," I said, my cheeks burning. "I should have paid better attention."

"You'll do better next time," Violet said, smiling at me.

Wow. I couldn't believe an eighth grader was even talking to me! Especially one who rode as well as Violet. Maybe she could teach me a few things.

Miss Cho walked into the arena and grinned at us. "Hi, everyone! If you'll space out your horses and do a sitting trot, we'll get started."

Violet dropped Hunter behind me and Charm. I followed Aaron and Rio, his strawberry roan mare.

I was NOT going to mess this one up. I stared between Charm's ears and took a deep breath. We circled the arena and Miss Cho watched each of us. When she looked at me, I sat up straighter and shoved my heels down as far as they would go.

"Now, move into a working trot, please."

Dressage wasn't my favorite discipline. Or Charm's

either. I'd complained about doing dressage earlier this year, but Callie had talked me into it. I sighed. The clinic would have been so much better if Callie weren't avoiding me.

"Miss Silver!" Miss Cho called.

I jerked my head up and looked at her. "Yes?"

She put her hands on her hips and frowned at me. "Do you notice anything?"

What? I looked around and everyone was still doing a working trot . . . OMG. They'd changed directions!

"I'm so sorry," I babbled. "I didn't hear you say to reverse."

"Clearly. Please follow instructions, Miss Silver."

I turned Charm in the opposite direction, humiliated. We passed Jasmine and she smirked.

"Oops," she mouthed.

This whole day had been a complete disaster. I'd messed up in front of *two* instructors and embarrassed myself and Charm. If Jasmine didn't already have a blog, she'd probably start one just to broadcast details of my embarrassing clinic mishaps.

The rest of the class seemed to take forever. We moved through several dressage exercises and Miss Cho noticed even the tiniest of errors. I forced myself not to think about Callie or Jacob again.

Finally, Miss Cho held up a hand. "All right. That's it for today. Please cool and untack your horses. When you're finished, come back to the arena for a quick meeting."

We dismounted and I sandwiched Charm between Aaron and Cole so Jasmine couldn't get near us.

I took Charm to the outer aisle of the stable and walked him up and down. I leaned my head against his neck. "That can't happen again, boy," I whispered. "I'm so sorry. We'll show them next time, I promise."

Charm snorted and reached his head around to nose my coat sleeve. I hugged him and hooked him up to cross-ties. I untacked him in record time and hurried to the arena. The sooner the meeting was over, the faster I could get out of here and forget this day ever happened.

The students trickled into the arena. No one said a word as Mr. Conner and the other instructors compared notes and talked.

Callie, Julia, and Alison stood together at the front of the arena. Why didn't Callie just change her name to Heather already?

Just then, the real Heather walked up and stood by me. "How was it?" she asked.

I shrugged. Heather wasn't my favorite person in the

world, but she *was* the only person on my team who was currently speaking to me. "Okay. You?"

"Easy," Heather said with a smile. "The riders in my class act as if they've never ridden before. One guy didn't even pay attention and I heard Ms. Thorne tell him she'll send him home if it happens again."

"Oh," I squeaked. Had Ms. Thorne thought that about me, too?

Heather and I turned to face the instructors as Mr. Conner began speaking. "I'll make this brief," he said. "This was, by far, the easiest day of this clinic. Things are only going to get more difficult. If you struggled today, you might want to speak with me or one of the other instructors about your continued participation."

I glanced around nervously, wanting to see if anyone else felt the way I did—terrified.

"If you still wish to continue, and I hope you all do, then you'll need to grab a handbook and go back to your dorms to study."

"Study?" Heather whispered to me.

I shrugged. Of course Canterwood found a way to inject school work into riding.

Mr. Bright stepped forward. "Please take one of these

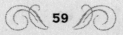

handbooks." He held up something that resembled a phone book. "For tomorrow's class with me, you'll need to have read the first three chapters about the history of the horse. Be prepared to answer questions."

"Joy," Heather said under her breath.

"And remember," Mr. Bright said. "The goal of this clinic is not just about teaching good riding skills, but also to inform you about horse care and proper nutrition for your equine friends. Happy studying!"

Each of the students stepped forward to take a handbook. Once I had mine, I immediately dodged Callie and Jasmine to get out of the room. I made it three feet out the door when I *finally* saw someone I didn't have to run away from.

"Eric!" I called.

He was kneeling next to one of the school horses and fixing a leg wrap. He looked nice in a brown and white crewneck sweater, dark brown breeches, and matching paddock boots.

"Hey," he said. He stood and smiled at me, his eyes meeting mine. "How was the first day?"

"Awful," I moaned. "I messed up SO many times."

"It couldn't have been that bad."

"I wish you were right. But it *was* that bad."

"Aw, sorry," Eric said. His eyes landed on my hand-book. "What's that?"

"Oh, we're supposed to read three chapters from this massive thing and be ready for questions tomorrow."

Eric took the handbook and paged through it. "Wow. You're going to learn a lot."

"I was wondering—and you totally don't have to—but if you want . . . maybe we could study together. We could both share my handbook and that way you'll learn, too. But if you're too busy, I understand."

"Sasha," Eric cut me off and grinned. "Of course I'll study with you. Studying horses isn't even like work."

"Cool," I said, relieved once again to have a friend. "Where do you want to meet?"

Eric handed me the book. "The Sweet Shoppe at six?"

"See you there."

7

SO NOT A DATE

I STOOD OUTSIDE THE SWEET SHOPPE AT 5:55 and looked around for Eric.

I couldn't help thinking about the time Jacob and I had stood on these steps. And how he'd always opened the door for me and let me pick the table. I had the sudden, over-whelming urge to call him. I dug my phone out of my pocket, found his number in my address book, and punched send.

"Hi, Sasha," Eric said behind me.

I jumped—paranoid much?—and looked at him before closing my phone and stuffing it into my bag. "Ready to study?" I asked. There. Done. I was going to study. NO JACOB.

"Sure." Eric opened the door for me and we stepped inside. "But how about we order something first?"

"Um, okay." But I was suddenly feeling less like this was a study session, and more like . . . well, Callie would have called it a date. But it *so* wasn't. I knew that. And Eric definitely knew that.

I mean, sure, he looked really cute tonight in his frayed dark-wash jeans and midnight blue polo sweater. And he *smelled* good—like his jacket, clean laundry and mint. But I was just being paranoid. I knew I was only thinking that way because Callie kept insisting it was true. And Eric had just been so nice to me. But I would never hurt Callie, even if she was being mean.

I calmed myself down with a few deep breaths and picked out a booth in the back of the shop—one without a window.

Eric plunked two notebooks and a handful of pens and highlighters on the table. "I probably brought enough for your entire class," he said with a laugh.

"You definitely did." I smiled, picking up a pink highlighter. Why did I feel so nervous all of a sudden?

"What do you want?" Eric asked. "I'm thinking hot chocolate and sugar cookies."

"That sounds great. But I'll order my own stuff."

But the last sentence wasn't out of my mouth before Eric stood and started for the counter. "It's no problem."

Okay, I'd *tried* to order for myself. I couldn't help it if he had manners.

I opened *The Young Rider's Equine Guide* and flipped to the first page. I selected one of Eric's notebooks and scribbled *Chapter One* at the top of the page.

"Here you go," Eric said, sliding a steaming pink mug in front of me.

He set a brown mug on his side of the table and put the cookie plate between us.

"Thanks. I'll pay you back," I said.

"You can get the next round." Eric laughed.

We sipped our drinks and I took a sweet, chewy bite of sugar cookie. *Yum.*

"So, how should we do this? You want to take turns reading aloud and then make notes?" I asked.

"Sure. You can read first."

I turned the book to me. "'The modern horse of today has progressed through many stages. The first animal to most resemble a horse was called a *Hyracotherium.*'"

I read to the halfway point of chapter one. "Let's stop and take notes," I said.

"Good idea," Eric said. "There are a lot of dates and Latin terms in that section."

Eric flagged the pages with dates while I started to

make a timeline of the horse's evolution. I chided myself for getting so worked up over nothing before. Callie had really gotten in my head! Eric was a great friend, and my study partner, and I was lucky for it.

We moved through the section quickly and then Eric took his turn reading. I half closed my eyes and listened to his voice. He was a good reader—not too fast or too slow. I'd bet he was a bookworm like me. While he read, I made notes on my paper.

I looked up when the door squeaked open and the little bell rang.

Heather and Ben walked through the shop hand in hand, and peered at the slices of pie in the glass display.

So she *was* with Ben. No wonder Julia and Alison had been ignoring her. I wondered if she'd faked going after Jacob so no one would pay attention to her *real* target—Ben.

Heather looked over her shoulder, saw me, and tucked a golden lock of hair behind her ear, almost nervously. Eric, oblivious to everything, kept reading. Then it came to me: Heather would probably run straight to Callie and tell her in a not-so-nice way that Eric and I had been together in the Sweet Shoppe. Ugh—I didn't even want to know what Heather's version of the story would be.

"Can you hold on a sec?" I interrupted Eric.

He stopped and looked up at me, inquiringly.

"Sorry," I said. "I need to talk to Heather for a minute."

"Heather?" he said, surprised. But then his expression changed. "Sure, I'll start highlighting notes for this chapter."

I got up and walked over to Heather.

"Hey," I said.

Ben peered around Heather and smiled at me. "Hey, Sasha." Heather whispered something to him and he said, "I'm going to look at the ice cream." He let go of Heather's hand and walked away.

"So, it *is* true," Heather said. She unbuttoned her red coat.

"Me and Eric? Nooo. It's not. See the books? We're *studying*. So don't run off to find Callie and tell her Eric and I are on a date. We're not."

Heather gave me an amused smile. "Do you think I care if you date or 'study' with Eric? Please. I'm not telling Harper anything."

Ben walked back over and put his arm around Heather's waist. "My parents should be here in an hour," he said. "They were supposed to pick me up yesterday, but they're a day late, like always."

"Have a good break," I said. *You jerk who dumped Julia for Heather!*

66

I stepped back and started for my table.

"Two oatmeal raisin cookies," Heather barked to the girl behind the counter. "And a caramel latte. Half skim, no sugar. Extra hot. Mine was cold last time."

The girl nodded furiously at Heather's directions and I headed back to my table, thinking about Jacob. About how we used to come to the Sweet Shoppe together, talking and laughing over frozen hot chocolates or cake.

I slid into my seat and tried to shake off the memory.

"Everything okay?" Eric asked.

"Yeah, fine. So, should we quiz each other now?" I shifted in my seat and looked at the book.

Eric must have realized I didn't want to talk. "Sure. I'll ask you first."

"Ready."

Eric closed his notebook and capped his green highlighter. With a grin, he pulled the book to his chest, reached across the table and swiped my notebook.

"Hey!" I protested.

"No cheating," Eric teased.

I mock-rolled my eyes and stuck my tongue out at him. "Fine, Mr. Rodriguez. Go ahead."

"All right. Who brought the first modern horses to America?"

"The Spaniards."

"Right. How many toes did the *Eohippus* have?"

I paused. "Four in the front . . . and three in the back?"

Eric frowned.

"Wait! Five in the front and four in the back?"

He laughed. "You were right the first time. I was just messing with you."

I kicked him under the table. "Mean."

"My turn." He slid the book to me.

I looked for the toughest question.

"Estimate how long ago the horse was domesticated."

"Five to six thousand years ago," Eric said without hesitation. "Is that all you've got?"

I smirked. "Okay . . . what was the first horselike animal with one hoof and no toes?"

Eric's face lost its cocky grin. "Uh. Hmm."

"Hmm? Did you say *hmm*?" I started to hum the *Jeopardy!* theme song.

Eric put his hands over his eyes. "The *Pliohippus*?"

"Yes." I sighed. "That's correct."

Eric reached out a hand and high-fived me. I giggled and sat back in my seat.

"Let's keep going," I said. "I'll read now." I wasn't ready to go back to my lonely room just yet.

8

AND BEST ACTRESS
GOES TO . . .

MR. CONNER'S CLINIC, DAY 2
HOURS SINCE CALLIE LAST SPOKE TO ME: 42

MR. CONNER MADE SURE THE RIDERS DIDN'T
waste one second of daylight during his clinic.

"Is it really seven in the morning during *break*?" I asked
Heather.

"Unfortunately."

We led our tacked-up horses down the aisle. Heather
and Aristocrat went to their group's class in the arena and
Charm and I headed to the outdoor arena.

We walked by Black Jack's stall. Callie stood outside
the door, texting. Again.

"Hi," I said, making the effort.

Charm stopped and stretched his neck toward Jack's

stall. Jack stuck his head over the door and touched noses with Charm.

Callie looked up and shoved her phone in her pocket. She'd done her hair a new way—a loose ponytail with the ends curled. It looked pretty.

"Whatever," she said.

I sighed, pulling Charm forward. She was never going to listen to me. And neither was Jacob. *Whatever* was right.

Once we got outside, I pulled on my red itchy wool gloves and zipped up my coat. The temperature hovered around forty degrees and the brightening sky was stark and cloudless.

Aaron, Violet, and Cole were already in the arena warming up their horses. Charm and I took a spot behind Aaron and Rio. We walked and trotted while we waited for Miss Cho.

Hoofbeats rang out over the yard and we all turned toward the sound. Jasmine and Phoenix cantered away from the stable and through the arena entrance. Did she *ever* give that horse a break? She fell into line behind Violet.

We rode in silence, except for the occasional snort from one of our horses, until Miss Cho walked into the arena. She looked pretty and professional in her sage-colored breeches, lace-up brown boots, and fitted black coat.

"Morning, everyone," she said. "If your horses are warmed up, let's get right to work. Today, I want to concentrate on flatwork. Please dismount."

Cole eyed me with a *what?* face and I shrugged. We all dismounted and stood beside our horses.

"We're going to play horse swap," Miss Cho said. "Cole, you take Aaron's horse. Aaron, you get Violet's. Sasha, take Jasmine's. Jasmine, you'll grab Charm. Violet, ride Cole's horse."

I bit back a groan as I handed Charm's reins to Jasmine. She was the *last* person I wanted to hold my horse.

Charm watched me as I walked away with Phoenix. The gray blew a friendly breath into my hand and leaned into me as I stroked his shoulder.

"Aw, you're a good guy, aren't you?" I asked Phoenix. He was *nothing* like Jasmine!

Once everyone finished swapping horses, we turned back to Miss Cho.

"All right, please mount your new horse and walk them until you get a feel for how they handle."

But! No! I didn't want Jasmine on my horse—especially after seeing the way she yanked Phoenix around and used her boots as weapons.

But before I could say no, Jasmine was in Charm's saddle. I noticed that she didn't even look to see if Phoenix was comfortable with me. I swung myself into Phoenix's saddle and walked him over to Charm. While we mounted, Mike and Doug set up five white skinny poles with weighted bases down the center of the arena.

"He has a *really* soft mouth," I told Jasmine. "He's sensitive to leg commands, too, so you shouldn't have to—"

"I know how to ride!" Jasmine said, shaking her head at me. "Besides, I've seen you ride him and whatever you're doing is definitely wrong. I can't wait to see how he does with a real rider."

If she even dared to kick Charm . . .

"Is everyone used to their new horses?" Miss Cho asked.

We nodded.

"Good. Then move your horses back to the arena entrance. We're going to be pole bending."

"Wait. *Pole bending?*" Violet sputtered. "Isn't that Western?"

Miss Cho adjusted the striped scarf around her neck. "Yes, it is. But pole bending is excellent for balance. It teaches a rider to maneuver a horse with their seat and legs, instead of heavy hands. Ready to get started?"

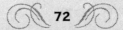

"Yes," we said in unison. I wouldn't take my eyes off Charm until Jasmine dismounted.

Forty-five minutes later, the lesson was over and we had swapped back to our own horses. Phoenix, calm under me, had been a perfect ride. I'd covered my eyes when Jasmine and Charm started their turn, but Jasmine knew just how to weave Charm through the poles.

"See? I didn't hurt your precious horse," Jasmine snipped, leading Phoenix away.

I hugged Charm and led him toward the exit.

"Not bad," Violet called to me.

"Thanks," I said. "I hope I'm as good as you are when I'm in eighth grade." I crossed my fingers that Violet wouldn't think I was a suck-up.

Violet pushed back her helmet and eyed me. "You better be."

She walked away before I could ask what she meant.

After Charm was cool, I untacked him, refilled his hay net and headed to the grain room for a session with Mr. Bright.

Cole, Aaron, Violet, and Jasmine were already in the room. I stood next to Violet and we watched as Mr. Bright finished pouring bran into five measuring cups.

"Welcome," Mr. Bright said to us. He looked the most relaxed of the instructors in khakis and Wellies. "Have any of you ever cooked for your horse before?"

Jasmine snorted and the rest of us shook our heads.

"Then you've been missing out," Mr. Bright said. "Proper nutrition is especially important to your horses in the winter months. Since it's almost spring, we want to feed them well to get them ready for spring shows, clinics, and other events."

He motioned for us to come closer to the wooden counter between us. "We're going to make hot bran mash for your horses. This is simple, and you can make it once a week if you like, as an extra treat."

OMG, Charm was going to *love* this! He'd probably never want another cold meal again.

"We're not going to make a full serving until we see if your horse likes it, but it'll be enough to teach you how to make it on your own," Mr. Bright said. "Each of you needs to grab a bucket."

I picked up a red one and put it in front of me.

"Now, pour your cup of bran into the bucket."

Jasmine covered a yawn. Cooking for Phoenix must have been low on her interest scale.

Mr. Bright put a tray of Thermoses on the counter.

Steam rose from the holes in the lids. "Carefully pour hot water over your bran and then stir with one of those wooden spoons."

I poured and started stirring. The bran started to soak up the water and it expanded in the bucket.

"Everyone okay?" Mr. Bright asked.

We nodded and kept stirring.

"While you stir, let's talk about last night's reading assignment," Mr. Bright said.

He could ask me anything—I was ready!

"Who can tell me when cave drawings of horses started to appear?" Mr. Bright asked.

Jasmine stared into her bucket and started stirring harder. Cole and Aaron looked at each other and shrugged.

"Around thirty thousand B.C.," I said.

"Yes, thank you, Sasha," Mr. Bright said. "Can anyone name one of the oldest horse breeds in the world?"

Silence. But I knew this—Eric had asked me this exact question last night.

I raised my hand slowly. Everyone was going to hate me for being Miss Know-It-All, but I'd studied hard.

"Sasha?" Mr. Bright asked.

"Arabians are one of the oldest breeds," I said. *Thank you, Eric.*

Jasmine glared at me and Violet stopped stirring to look at me.

"Correct again. Since no one else appears to have read the assigned material, I'll stop with the questions for now. After my session, I'll need Cole, Violet, Aaron, and Jasmine to go back to your dorms, read the chapters and come by my office before six to answer some more questions."

Jasmine huffed under her breath. I hid my smile and kept stirring.

Mr. Bright put a bowl of grated carrots in the middle of the counter.

"Everyone, take a handful of carrot and put that in your bucket. Then stir again."

I waited for Violet to grab her carrots before I took mine.

"Does anyone know why hot bran mash is good for most horses?" Mr. Bright asked.

Violet raised her hand and Mr. Bright nodded to her.

"It warms them up on cold days and it has lots of fiber," Violet said.

"Good, Violet," Mr. Bright said.

The grain room warmed from the steaming buckets of mash and the ends of my hair started to curl from the humidity. At least I hadn't messed mine up yet. I'd have to thank Paige later for giving me cooking confidence!

"Last step," Mr. Bright said. "Measure a couple of spoonfuls of molasses and stir that into your bucket. The mash will be warm when you serve it, but it cannot be hot. So, we'll have to let it sit for a few minutes after we're finished."

Mr. Bright put an almost empty bottle of molasses on the table and frowned. "That's not enough. Let me look in the cabinets and see if Mr. Conner has a new bottle in here."

He walked to the end of the grain room and rummaged through the cabinets. Finally, he came back with an unopened bottle and handed it to Jasmine. "Go ahead and measure yours."

"Mr. Bright?" Cole asked. "I think my mash looks . . . weird."

Mr. Bright moved down the table to Cole's blue bucket and looked inside.

Jasmine unscrewed the cap on the bottle and shifted her bucket over, knocking my handbook off the table.

"Oops," she said, tilting her head. "Sorry."

"You don't look sorry," I muttered. I leaned over to pick up my book. Then something . . . *sticky* dripped on my neck and oozed onto my hair.

I gasped and straightened. I swiped at my neck and came away with a gross brown blob of molasses!

"Jasmine!" I screamed. "What's your problem?"

Jasmine grinned and folded her arms. "Oh, no, Sasha! I'm *so* clumsy today."

Mr. Bright hurried over and looked at us. "Girls! What happened?"

Jasmine's smile faded and she put a hand to her forehead. "Mr. Bright, I'm so, so sorry. I . . ." She sat on a stack of grain bags along the wall. "I have low blood sugar sometimes. It has been especially bad today. I've tried to hide it because I don't want to waste one day of learning. But when I went to pour the molasses into my bucket, I got dizzy. Sasha was bending down beside me and I accidentally spilled it on her."

Wow. Jasmine's acting skills put Heather's to shame. Jasmine turned to me, her bottom lip quivering. "I'm so sorry, Sasha. I'll dry-clean your coat or something. Anything! I just feel terrible."

Gag me. I looked at Mr. Bright—there was no way he could believe her.

"Sasha, you may be excused to go get cleaned up. I'll make sure your horse gets his mash."

"Yes, sir," I said.

"Jasmine, you may also leave to go see the school nurse," Mr. Bright said. "We need to make sure that you're all right."

"Okay, Mr. Bright," Jasmine said in a faint tone.

She started to ease herself up off the grain bag and practically limped to the door.

"And Jasmine?" Mr. Bright said.

She turned back. "Yes?"

"I think it would be best if you skipped riding the rest of today. Stay with the school nurse until you're well and then please go back to your dorm. You can use that time to read and study. Jumping would be too dangerous for you today."

Ha! I smiled at Jasmine.

She mashed her lips together and slammed the door on her way out. Her limp had vanished. Shocker.

Mr. Bright winked at me. "Go change," he said.

I grabbed my handbook off the floor and practically skipped back to Winchester.

9

CLICK

IT TOOK TWICE THE NORMAL AMOUNT OF strawberry smoothie–scented shampoo to get the molasses out of my hair. When I finally got it out, I put on a pair of fresh breeches and a green and gold Canterwood hooded sweatshirt. I quickly fastened my molasses-free hair back into a French braid.

On a whim, I turned on my laptop. I checked my e-mail and stared at my empty inbox.

Suddenly, I had the overwhelming urge to e-mail Jacob. I'd tried calling him several times now, but every time, I chickened out.

I got up and paced around my dorm. It seemed easier to write an e-mail than call, but what if it only made things worse? I refreshed my browser. *Zero unread messages.* I wished Paige was around. She would know what to tell me.

I finally bit my lip and started typing. If I got done and decided not to send it, I wouldn't have to. There was no harm in just typing it, was there?

Dear Jacob,
I've wanted to talk to you since the Sweetheart Soirée, but . . . I don't know. I guess, honestly, I haven't tried that hard. I've been too afraid that you'd walk away again or would ignore me or something.

Part of me kind of thought that you'd e-mail, or text, or call me, and I wouldn't have to. Yeah, I know—most of this was my fault because I believed Heather over you. And I should have talked to you more when I was worried about Heather to begin with. I didn't.

But you could have told me that you did school stuff with her sometimes. I know you're not a mind reader, but you knew Heather and I didn't get along. You also could have at least given me a chance to apologize.

So I guess I'm just really sad that we don't talk anymore. I wish we did! I had so much fun with you and, you know, liked you. Okay, I'm finally saying it: I. Like. You. A lot. And I thought you maybe liked me, too. If you want to talk, maybe you'll e-mail me back. I hope so.
~Sasha

I reread the e-mail at least a hundred times. It was what I'd been wanting to say to him for forever. I just never had the guts to do it. And now that I had, it felt really good.

I saved the e-mail to my drafts folder, but left it open on the screen. Should I send it? I meant every word. And if he didn't want to e-mail me back, he didn't have to. Then I'd know it was definitely over and at least I'd tried.

I moved the mouse over the send button. I got up and walked the length of the room.

"Just send it," I said to myself. "Press the button and send it."

I made another trip back and forth across the room before I stood over the computer.

Before I could change my mind, I grabbed the mouse, hovered over send and closed my eyes. *Click.*

I opened one eye and looked at the screen.

Message sent.

The e-mail was gone. I couldn't take it back. My feelings about Jacob were out there now.

I slammed the laptop closed, grabbed my handbook off my bed, and plopped on my bed and started reading. That lasted all of about five minutes. Maybe I could check my e-mail . . .

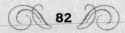

I opened the laptop and pulled up my e-mail. *Zero unread messages.*

Yeah, that would have been awful fast. Back to reading. But soon, the words on the page blurred and every other word looked like *Jacob*.

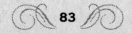

10

MEET THE BELLES

MR. CONNER'S CLINIC, DAY 3
MINUTES SINCE I E-MAILED JACOB: 1,320

WEDNESDAY MORNING WAS PERFECT. JUST Charm and me. The students had the morning off. By "off," Mr. Conner meant grooming horses, cleaning tack, or mucking stalls. I didn't mind—I was glad to spend time with Charm.

My phone buzzed—a text from Eric. *Mr. C trying 2 kill me. Making me alphabetize horse meds & vitamins.*

I started laughing and texted back. *Ugh! Sorry. :(*

I smoothed the body brush over Charm's glistening chestnut coat and flicked the last bit of straw off his leg. I knelt down and lifted his foreleg to check his hoof for dirt. Clean.

Boots tapped down the aisle and stopped beside me. I looked up. Violet's hair was styled into soft waves and the lack of horsehair on her clothes suggested she hadn't touched a horse all morning. I ran my fingers through my messy hair and smiled at her.

"Hi," I said.

"You almost done?" she asked.

"Yeah . . . do you need the crossties?"

Violet reached around me to pat Charm. "No. Meet me in the hayloft in ten minutes."

She was gone before I had a chance to ask why.

Charm went eagerly into his stall, hungry after being away from his hay net for thirty minutes. I put his tack box away and took my time walking down the aisle.

I looked around to be sure Mr. Conner or one of the other instructors wasn't watching. The aisle was clear. I climbed the wooden ladder up to the hayloft and almost bumped into Callie. She looked at me, and not in the I-still-hate-you kind of way.

"Hey," I said.

Callie opened her mouth, but before she could say anything, Julia and Alison jumped up from the hay bale they'd been sitting on and walked behind Callie.

"What do *you* want?" Alison asked.

"I just said hi to *Callie*," I said.

"Well, don't," Julia said. "She doesn't want to talk to you. Obviously."

"Move!" a voice said behind me.

I jumped out of the way as Heather came up the ladder. She shook her head when she saw Julia, Alison, Callie, and me. "Why are we here?"

"I'll explain," said Violet as she and two other girls walked out from behind the massive stack of hay bales. "Have a seat." She motioned for us to sit.

"These are my friends, Brianna and Georgia," she added. "We're on the eighth-grade advanced team."

"Oh!" Julia said. She pulled off her crème colored beret—which she claimed her father got her on a business trip to Paris—and sat up straighter. "You're the Belles."

Violet smiled at Julia. "Smart girl. If you haven't heard of us by now, then you're in the wrong circle."

Callie and I glanced at each other before looking back at Violet. I'd never heard of them and the look on Callie's face made me think she hadn't either.

"Belles?" Callie asked. "Are you all from the South or something?"

Brianna, a petite girl with short, choppy black hair, scrunched up her nose. "Violet—she's from Nashville,

Georgia's from DC, and I'm from Virginia."

"*Anyway,*" Violet said, looking at her friends. "We asked you here because Canterwood needs the *best* riders showing on behalf of our school. Next fall, we'll be in ninth grade, representing Canterwood in competitions for high school. You'll be in our old slots—the faces of Canterwood's younger team."

Violet picked a stalk of hay out of a bale next to her and twirled it in her fingers. She looked at Georgia.

"We want Canterwood's reputation to remain strong," Georgia said. "We can't have anyone on the advanced team who isn't fully committed to being here."

"And that's up to you?" Heather questioned.

Julia and Alison's eyes widened and they inched away from Heather.

Violet laughed. "Of course not! Mr. Conner picked you for his seventh-grade team because he knows you're good riders. We just want to make sure that Canterwood is number one."

"Meet us tomorrow under the stone arch at the far side of the courtyard at sundown," Brianna said mysteriously.

Before we could ask any questions, the Belles stood and climbed down the ladder. Something told me this was going to be interesting.

"See you tomorrow!" Heather said in a fake cheery tone as she left the loft. Julia, Alison, Callie, and I followed Heather down the ladder.

Callie stopped in the aisle when her phone beeped. *Message from*—that's all I saw before Callie shifted, having caught me looking.

"What?" she asked, clicking the phone shut.

"Nothing," I said.

We split up and I went to Charm's stall to get him ready for lessons with our fave instructor, Ms. Thorne.

"Sasha, more leg! Keep your hands steady! Stop jerking on Charm's mouth!"

Ms. Thorne had been barking out commands like that for the past half hour. And I hadn't been listening. Yes, I wanted to have steady hands and firmer leg signals, but my mind wouldn't stay on the lesson. On top of the fact that I *had* to know whether or not Jacob had e-mailed me back, tomorrow's meeting with the Belles sounded so totally suspicious.

I looked ahead at the jump. Ms. Thorne had been making my group take turns. Jasmine had been perfect. Violet's eyes had followed Jasmine—I wondered if she wished Jasmine went to Canterwood instead of me.

Before I could even clear my head, Charm was already strides away from the vertical. His canter slowed, but there wasn't enough time. He dug his heels into the arena dirt and slid to a halt, his muzzle just inches away from the rail. My feet came out of the stirrups and I slid up on his withers.

"Charm!"

He backed away, shaking his head and ignoring my voice.

The last time Charm had refused a jump . . . I couldn't even remember!

"Bring Charm around, circle him a couple of times and take him over the jump again," Ms. Thorne said. "You must pay attention, Sasha. You both could have been seriously hurt."

I nodded. This wasn't supposed to happen! Show jumping was *my* thing—Charm and I were better than this.

I took a couple of shaky breaths and let Charm canter in a wide circle.

Charm eased out of the circle and I watched the vertical's red and yellow rails get closer. I started counting strides early. *Five, four, three, two, one, and now!* I lifted out of the saddle, squeezed my legs against Charm's sides and gave him rein. He rocketed into the air, cleared the rail and landed softly on the other side.

"Good boy!" I said. I patted his neck and looked over at Ms. Thorne.

"Much better," Ms. Thorne said. "Cole, go ahead."

Charm and I headed to join our group, relieved. But the more I thought about Callie, Jacob, and the Belles, the worse Charm and I did. It had to stop. I closed my eyes for a second, blocking out all of the stuff from the past few days, and then opened them. Charm snorted and I rubbed his neck.

"I'm with you, boy," I whispered.

Ms. Thorne turned to face all of us. "Good work, everyone," she said. "That's it for today. Please cool your horses and I'll see you tomorrow."

I sat back in the saddle and slowed Charm to a walk.

Jasmine rode Phoenix beside us and pushed her helmet back. "How did you even make the seventh-grade advanced team?"

I kept my eyes forward. "How did you even get an invite to this clinic?"

Jasmine let Phoenix drop behind Charm. We walked for fifteen minutes before he felt cool enough to go back to his stall. My legs wobbled and I couldn't wait to get back into my dorm and curl up in bed with a book.

"Tough lesson?"

I looked up and saw Eric. I noticed that, even at the stable, he always looked nice. Today, he wore dark jeans and a long-sleeved red henley. I suddenly felt self-conscious about my dirty breeches and sawdust-covered boots.

"The worst," I said. "I was awful. Charm ran out on a jump and Ms. Thorne made us hold our jump seats for the longest time."

"Sorry." Eric winced. He walked with me toward Charm's stall. "Want me to untack Charm and put him away for you?"

"No way, I couldn't ask you to do that. It won't take me long."

"No, really. I don't mind," Eric said. "No offense, but you look tired."

I put my free hand on my hip and pretended to look annoyed. "Okay, first you call me heavy and now you're saying I look tired. Thanks a lot!"

Eric laughed and I couldn't hide my smile.

"Okay," I said. "I *am* tired. If you're sure you don't mind, I promise I'll put Luna away for you sometime."

"No worries," Eric said. He reached over and took Charm's reins from my hands. "Now go."

"Going," I said. "Thanks. I owe you."

I turned and walked down the aisle. I didn't trust

Charm with many people, but he'd be safe with Eric. I got a few feet down the aisle when I spotted Callie.

"Yeah, Sash," she said, looking up at me from her phone. "You're really not with Eric. That's *so* clear."

I shrugged. "You never believe me about Eric, so I'm not going to bother saying it again."

I'd explained enough. I left Callie behind and walked out the door without a second glance.

After I showered, I checked my e-mail for the millionth time. *Nothing* from Jacob. Not a "Got your message" or "I'll call you." I'd even settle for a "I never want to talk to you again!!" at this point. Anything!

I turned on iChat and crossed my fingers that Paige was online. She was!

"Hey!" I said.

"Sasha!" Paige squealed. Her red hair hung in pretty waves around her shoulders and she wore a cropped lavender cardigan that tied in the front.

"Did you swipe those earrings from the *Teen Cuisine* set?" I teased.

Paige touched the silver chandelier earrings. "Not exactly. I can borrow a few things if I sign them out and take them back the next day."

"That's so cool! Maybe I'll bail on the clinic and become your groupie."

"Bail? Why?"

I groaned. "Callie hates me, Jacob won't e-mail me back, this girl Violet is being super shady, and Jasmine wants me kicked out of the clinic."

"Wait, you e-mailed Jacob? When?"

"Yesterday." I checked my e-mail again. "Still nothing."

"Maybe he's too busy to check e-mail," Paige said. "He could be somewhere with his family or something."

"Maybe."

Paige leaned closer to the camera. "I'm sorry, Sash. You could call him or text him, you know. Or just give him space and let him come to you."

I played with a fuzzy blue pen from my desk. "I'll wait. For now."

"If I were there, I'd so bake you a pie right now!" Paige said.

"Like your chocolate mousse pie with whipped cream?"

"*And* homemade crust," Paige added.

Mmmm.

"Oh! Guess what? *I* made something today! Your culinary genius has rubbed off on me."

Paige clapped her hands together. "No! What did you

make? Lemon meringue pie? Raspberry chocolate cake?"

"Um, no," I said, laughing. "I made hot bran mash!"

Paige got still. "What?"

"Hot bran mash for Charm. One of my instructors taught me."

Paige didn't blink. "The first real meal you made was for . . . *Charm*?"

I nodded.

Paige burst into giggles. "I have *not* taught you well! It's cooking lessons for you when I get back!"

I grinned back at her and let her distract me with all of the recipes she was going to teach me. Paige talked about so many cake, torte, and pudding recipes that for a few minutes, I forgot all about my empty inbox.

In fact, it was decided. I wasn't going to be *that* girl who pined over a boy—starting now.

II

SPELL "EMBARRASSED": S-A-S-H-A

MR. CONNER'S CLINIC, DAY 4
DAYS TILL DEMO: 9
(NOTE THE TOTAL LACK OF MENTION OF THE J-WORD)

THE SKY WAS STILL DARK WHEN I GOT TO THE stable on Thursday morning. Last night, it had taken forever to get to sleep. All I could think about was the mysterious meeting with the Belles.

Right now, I didn't even care about running into Callie. I just wanted tonight to hurry up and get here so I could meet Violet and her friends. I grabbed Charm's tack box and walked to his stall, passing Heather who had Aristocrat tied to the iron bars on his stall.

"Hi, rock star!" I said.

He popped his head over the stall door and let me kiss his muzzle.

"Today's going to be better, boy. No distractions—I promise."

Charm eyed me with suspicion, but let me lead him out of the stall and down the aisle to a free set of crossties by Aristocrat's stall.

Aristocrat raised his head when he saw Charm. Charm lifted his muzzle higher into the air and snorted. Boys.

"So . . ." I said to Heather. "Are you nervous about tonight?"

She kept brushing Aristocrat's flank.

"Okay. Forget it." I grabbed a hoof pick, leaned against Charm's shoulder and started picking dirt out of his hoof.

When I stood, Heather was beside me. I jumped.

"Hello! Say something next time you decide to sneak up on someone," I said. "What?"

Heather looked over her shoulder and then back at me. "Nothing. Well, I'm only telling you this because you're pathetic and I feel sorry for you but . . . the Belles have a reputation around here."

I decided to ignore the comment about me being pathetic. "Like what kind of reputation?"

"If you stop interrupting, I'll tell you!" Heather snapped.

I closed my mouth.

"Violet, Brianna, and Georgia are known for being risky riders. They'll do *whatever* it takes to make sure other schools know they're the best."

"Like Jasmine?"

Heather gave me a withering look. "Not even close." She walked back to Aristocrat. "You'll see for yourself."

Please. Like I believed her. She was probably trying to freak me out so I didn't go. Then there would be one less person competing for the Belles' attention. Not. Gonna. Happen.

I began brushing Charm and then looked up at the sound of my name.

"Sasha," Miss Cho said. She walked up to us and patted Charm's shoulder. "Don't tack up. Put a cavesson on Charm and come to the round pen."

"Okay," I said, suspicious. "Think my group's going to lunge?" I asked Heather. I hadn't lunged Charm in months.

"No, she's making you get the cavesson for nothing, Silver," she said, rolling her eyes. "Go grab it. I'll watch Charm."

"Thanks."

I hurried to the tack room and came back with a cavesson, which was like a halter with extra rings across the noseband. The headpiece was lined so the horse didn't get sores from the pressure. I buckled the cavesson on Charm and led him out to the round pen. Jasmine was already waiting. Violet, leading Hunter, stopped beside Charm and the three—wait, six—of us waited in silence for Cole, Aaron, and Miss Cho to arrive.

Cole and Aaron, both in black breeches, led their horses up to the round pen. This pen was the biggest I'd ever seen. It was a sixty-foot pen with a dome top. Most of the round pens I'd used with Charm had metal rails with peeling orange or red paint. The pens had been less than half the size of this one and had no top. I loved standing in the center of the pen and watching Charm circle me—I got to see exactly how he moved.

"Lunging?" Aaron guessed.

"I think so," I said. "It'll be different."

"Yeah," Cole added. "I've never lunged before."

Jasmine's head twisted toward him. "You've never worked your horse from the ground on a lunge line before?"

Cole shook his head. "Nope."

"Ugh, I *am* with a group of losers," Jasmine said.

Violet stepped forward, hand jutting out from her hip. "*Excuse* me?"

"Sorry," Jasmine muttered quickly.

That was weird, I thought. What did *Jasmine* care what Violet thought? It wasn't like Jasmine even went to Canterwood.

"Hi, class," Miss Cho said. She held a coiled lunge line in one hand and a lunge whip in the other. "Let's get started. I asked you to leave your horses untacked because we're going to lunge today. You'll each take turns standing in the center of the round pen and lunging your horse."

"Why are we lunging today?" Cole asked.

"Well," Miss Cho said. "Because when you're riding your horse, it's impossible for you to see how the horse moves. Sure, you can feel it, but you can't see it. You'll get a new perspective from the ground today. I know this is a new practice for many of you—but don't worry. I'll show you how."

I looked over at Aaron and smiled. This would be fun!

"Who *has* lunged before?" Miss Cho asked.

I raised my hand. "I have."

Miss Cho nodded at me. "Okay, then you may go first.

Bring Charm inside. The rest of you, lead your horses closer to the round pen and watch."

I led Charm forward and we stepped through the narrow gate and into the round pen. The metal rails were six feet high and the bottom four feet had a solid plastic shield so a horse couldn't get caught up on the rail.

Miss Cho closed the gate behind us and I stopped Charm beside her. She clipped the lunge line to a ring on Charm's cavesson and handed it to me.

"How do you hold the line and the whip?" she asked.

"If we go to the left, I hold the line in my left hand and the whip in my right," I said.

"Correct. Good. Go ahead and give him line and ask him to walk."

Miss Cho stood by me as I fed Charm a bit of line and moved the whip behind his hindquarters. He started forward and walked out to the rail.

I kept tension in the line and watched as Charm circled at a walk.

"How does his stride look to you?" Miss Cho asked.

"Good," I said. "His walk looks fine to me."

"I agree. Ask him to trot."

"Charm," I said, projecting my voice over the pen. "Trot!"

I kept the whip lowered, but snapped it into the dirt. Charm trotted. I watched his legs move and turned slowly when I passed Jasmine. She rolled her eyes.

Charm trotted several laps around the pen. "Where could Charm improve with his trot?" Miss Cho asked.

I studied his movements. "His stride looks a little short," I said. "Maybe I should work with him on extension?"

"Great idea, Sasha," Miss Cho said. "Now, let's ask him to canter."

"Charm, canter!" I called. Charm ignored me and continued to trot. "Canter." I snapped the whip along the ground and Charm bolted forward.

"Easy!" The line jerked on my hands and Charm tugged me forward. I stumbled and dug my heels into the dirt to keep Charm from pulling me along with him. "Charm, slow," I said.

But he didn't listen. His stride quickened and his hooves pounded the dirt. I dropped the whip and started to wrap the line around my hand.

"Don't do that," Miss Cho cautioned. "If he bolts again, he could drag you. Shorten the line and force him to make smaller circles. He can't keep up that pace if the circle is smaller. He'll lose his balance."

All I could do was nod. I watched Charm canter around me and I tugged six inches of line toward me. It pulled on Charm's head and he slowed a fraction.

"Take it in again," Miss Cho said.

I gathered more line and—thankfully—Charm's canter finally eased away from a gallop.

"Keep him at this pace for another lap and then bring him down to a trot," Miss Cho said.

Charm cantered smoothly around the pen. When he'd made a full circle, I called out, "Trot."

Within four strides, he slowed to a trot. My sharp breaths eased back to normal.

"Ask him to walk," Miss Cho said.

I couldn't look at her. I wasn't even able to control Charm during an easy exercising like lunging!

"Sasha, you did an excellent job handling him during that bolt," Miss Cho said. "Remember, Charm *does* have Thoroughbred in him. He's a sensitive horse and spooks happen. Half the battle is knowing how to control them. Good job."

I nodded my thanks and led Charm out of the pen. I walked him in small circles to cool him.

"Aaron, come on in," Miss Cho said.

Charm nosed my coat and nudged my pockets for

a treat. "No way," I said. "You have to behave to get a treat."

I crossed my arms and watched the rest of my group lunge their horses. Charm kept inching closer to me, trying to make up for the lunging disaster, but I ignored him. I chewed on the inside of my cheek to keep from crying. I kept messing up—it wasn't Charm's fault. But I'd been taking it out on him.

"Sorry," I whispered. I hugged him and leaned my head on his shoulder. "I'll give you a treat later."

Charm looked at me with his big brown eyes and he rubbed his head up and down on my arm. I smiled. That was my boy!

12

GET THE HORSES A CHAPERONE

AFTER CLASS, I LED CHARM AROUND THE YARD to cool him out. I had an idea. I halted him and pulled out my phone. *Walking Charm outside. If ur not busy, bring Luna and walk w us.*

My phone buzzed a few seconds later. *On r way!*

Charm and I waited for Eric and Luna. Charm gave a throaty nicker when he saw Luna coming over the hill.

"I'm glad you texted," Eric said. "Luna needed to get out of her stall, but I didn't have time to ride her today. A walk is better than nothing."

"Definitely." I patted Luna's neck. "Hi, girl."

"Hello, sir," Eric said to Charm. He rubbed Charm's shoulder.

"Want to walk over by the lake?" I asked.

"Sure."

Our boots crunched over the dead grass and we fell into stride beside each other. Charm craned his neck to look at the turned out horses—bundled in quilted blankets—that grazed in the far pasture. The pasture's dark brown fences seemed to stretch for miles.

"It's like we're the only people on campus," Eric said.

"I love Canterwood like this," I said. "Calm, quiet. It's so peaceful."

We walked past the closed tennis courts and the gym. We were allowed to walk the horses around campus if we kept them on the outer edge, off the sidewalks, and away from buildings.

It felt good to get away from the stable and the popular hangout spots for a while. Even though it was cold outside, the sun warmed my face and soaked warmth into my winter layers.

"How was the lesson?" Eric asked. "You've still got a cavesson on Charm."

"Miss Cho had us lunge our horses. Charm bolted and almost galloped in the round pen."

Eric glanced at me. "Did you drop the line?"

"No."

"Slip and fall?"

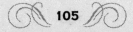

"No . . ."

"Did Miss Cho throw you out of the pen?"

"No! None of that happened. Oh." I smiled. "So, you're trying to tell me whatever happened wasn't *that* bad."

"Exactly."

"True, it could have been worse. But something is off. Charm bolted and, a while ago, he refused a jump. He doesn't do that stuff. Why now?"

Eric adjusted his grip on Luna's blue lead line. "Maybe because you're both stressed. Plus, with the new students and different teachers, you probably both need an adjustment period."

We reached the tiny lake on the far side of campus and stopped the horses. The thawed lake was clear. Water lapped the smooth rounded stones that lined the shoreline.

"When it gets hot out, I'm taking Charm wading," I said.

Eric grinned. He pointed to low-hanging tree branch on an oak tree a few feet away. "Want to tie them there and walk out on the dock?"

"Sure."

We tied Luna and Charm with slipknots and walked out on the wooden dock.

106

"The lake looks so pretty in the winter," I said. I crouched down and sat on my heels. "I like it when the water's clear and it doesn't have any of that gross algae on top."

Eric nodded and sat beside me. "It's good to be away from everyone sometimes."

My thoughts exactly.

"How's Mr. Conner been—as a boss I mean?" I asked.

"He's been great, actually," Eric said. "I thought he'd make me do a lot of tough chores, but he has been letting me watch a ton of classes. I told him we'd studied the handbook together and he liked that."

"Oooh! We'll have to study again soon. I completely forgot with everything that's been going on. I got lucky that Miss Cho didn't ask us any questions today."

Eric glanced behind us, checking on the horses. "Um, I think our horses need a chaperone."

"What?" I turned and looked at Charm and Luna.

The horses had moved so they were muzzle to muzzle. Charm blew in Luna's nostrils and their heads were together.

"That's so cute!" I said.

Eric looked at me. "I think someone has a crush."

"Charm's in *loooove* with Luna."

"Yeah," Eric said after a second. "Charm and Luna."

13

WITH US
OR AGAINST US

I LOOKED OUT MY WINDOW AT THE PINK, purple, and orange—tinged sky. Sundown was minutes away.

I pulled on a brown hooded tweed coat over a ribbed pink ballet top and stepped into my favorite skinny jeans. For the finishing touch, I shoved my feet into a new pair of soft brown ankle boots. There. For once, the Belles wouldn't see me in my stable slob clothes. I didn't want to lie to Livvie about where I was going, so I sneaked past her office and eased open the dorm door.

I hunched against the cold as I left Winchester. The shadowy lawn looked eerie in the stark silence of the empty campus. I was relieved when I saw Julia already waiting under the arch. I took a breath and walked up to her. Julia rolled her eyes and looked straight ahead—away from me.

But I ignored the diss. I was glad for a chance to talk with no one else around. "Why are you guys acting like this?" I asked.

"Like what?" Julia asked innocently.

"Like I stole Eric from Callie."

"Didn't you?" she sneered.

"Who even told you that?" I asked. "Did Callie?"

Julia folded her arms. "So what if she did?"

"It's not true!" I said. "I'm *not* with Eric. I keep telling her that and she doesn't believe me. All I want is to get Jacob back."

Julia tilted her head. "You want Jacob back?"

"Yes!"

"Whatever," Julia said, shaking her head. "I don't believe you. At least Callie and I understand each other. We both got burned—by you and Heather."

I wanted to scream at her.

"Hi, Julia," Callie said, coming over to us. She moved between Julia and me. We didn't say anything else as we waited for Alison, Heather, and the Belles.

Alison and Heather showed up at almost the same

time. We huddled under the arch, keeping our bodies away from the freezing stone.

"They should have been here by now," Alison grumbled, hopping up and down for warmth. "It's almost completely dark."

The sky had lost its sherbet colors. The pink had turned to a deep purplish red and the blue was almost black. The temperature felt as though it was dropping by the minute, and the stone arch didn't provide any warmth—only protection from the wind.

"It's part of their game," Heather said.

"What if a teacher catches us out here?" Julia whispered.

We could barely see one another's faces in the dark. I was too nervous about being caught to use my cell as a flashlight.

We waited. And waited. Then guess what? More waiting!

Crack! Something crashed around us and clattered onto the stone under our feet.

"Ahh!" We screamed and grabbed each other's arms. I held my breath—too scared to make a sound. We backed out of the archway.

"What . . . was that?" Callie asked, her voice shaking.

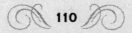

A light flashed on. Julia, clutching her cell, held it in front of us and the light spilled over the stone.

"There's something on the ground." I pointed to an object a few feet away.

Julia aimed her cell in that direction. "Alison!" she yelled.

"What?" Alison asked. She peered where Julia pointed the light.

"Oh. Oops. Sorry." Alison jogged under the arch and bent down. She picked up something and came back. "My mirror fell out of my pocket."

We all groaned.

"That's it," Heather said. "Five more minutes and I'm out of here."

"Me too," I said. "This is ridiculous."

A light wind started to blow. I shivered, moving back under the protection of the arch, and everyone stepped inside with me. Ivy, frostbitten by the cold, grew in tangled spirals out of the rock and looked as if it was trying to choke the stone.

"They're not coming," Heather said. "They just did this to—"

"To what?" asked a voice behind us.

We jumped and turned around. A flashlight clicked on

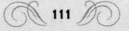

and it lit ghostly shadows on Violet's face. She held it under her chin. Two more flashlights flickered on, revealing Brianna and Georgia beside Violet. All three girls wore dark coats and pants.

"If you're finished freaking out, you can follow us," Violet said.

Heather mumbled something under her breath, but we bunched together and followed the girls through the stone archway. It was too dark to see the opening at the other end of the tunnel. The Belles stopped halfway through and Brianna aimed her flashlight at the wall.

I stepped closer to see what they were doing. More ivy grew along the inside wall. Georgia pushed it aside with a gloved hand and ran her fingers along the wall.

"What are you looking for?" Julia asked.

"Shhh!" Callie said. "Someone will hear us."

Violet laughed. "Please. There's no one out here. It's just us."

"More light," Georgia said.

Brianna moved closer to the wall and pointed the flashlight at Georgia's hands.

"Got it!" Georgia said with a grin. "Key, please?"

She kept one hand on the wall and held out her free hand to Violet.

Violet reached into her pocket and pulled a long, intricate key from her pocket. The silver key had loops and twists on the top and it was the length of Violet's hand.

Georgia stuck the key into the keyhole and turned the brass doorknob. She pushed on the door and waved a hand at Brianna. "A little help?" she asked.

Brianna pushed her shoulder against the door. It opened into a black room.

Brianna, Georgia, and Violet stepped into the blackness. I looked at Callie. The fear in her eyes was visible. But she pushed back her shoulders and walked into the room. That was Callie—she never backed down from anything.

"C'mon!" Violet insisted. "I'd like to do this before midnight, if possible."

Alison and Julia grabbed each other's hands and walked through the doorway.

Together, Heather and I were the last ones to hurry through the doorway. The flashlights went off, the door slammed behind us and I stood in the dark listening to blood pump in my ears.

A few feet away, a tiny flame ignited. Violet held a match in her hand and reached up to light candles in

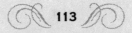

fixtures mounted to the wall that staggered up to the ceiling. Georgia and Brianna struck matches and lit candles on a table in the center of the room. As light filled the space, I looked around. Two tapers flickered on a round table in the center of the room.

"What is this place?" Alison asked, releasing Julia's hand.

"It used to be a meeting room for Canterwood officials," Violet said. "They stopped using it fifty years ago when they built the new admissions building."

"How'd you get a key?" Callie said.

Violet smiled. "Questions later. For now, let's sit."

We walked up to the table. Carvings of ivy spiraled up the table legs. I ran my finger along the table's edge. Unlike most of the other dust-covered surfaces in the room, it had been wiped clean. The wooden chairs surrounding the table had been as well. The Belles must have come here before the meeting.

I pulled out a chair and the scraping of chair legs against the stone screeched in the small room. I took a seat next to Heather and Alison. Julia sat on Alison's other side and Callie took a chair by her. I kept glancing at the door. Any second, a teacher could find us in here. We'd all be kicked out for sure.

Violet shifted the tapers out of the way so she could see our faces across the table.

"We asked you to come here tonight because we wanted to speak with you privately," Violet said.

"We've already told you that we're graduating to high school next year," Brianna said. "We'll still be Canterwood students, but we won't represent the middle school riders. We need friends who can."

"And do it well," Georgia added. "We want *all* of Canterwood's advanced teams to be fierce. Students should hear our school's name and know we're number one."

A look passed among the Belles.

Violet folded her hands and looked at us. "Before you all start on Canterwood's eighth-grade advanced team, we'll have Initiation," she said. "If you participate, as we did when we were in your place, we will advise you during your eighth-grade year. We'll help you meet the right people and get invites to the coolest parties, and we'll make sure you're the best riders."

Parties, people, and riding: good.

Initiation: bad.

Violet must have sensed nerves coming from our end of the table. "But don't worry!" she said with a smile. "If

you don't want our help, then you're free to leave. Right now. Get up and walk out the door."

Silence.

No one moved. My stomach swirled and I knew I should get up and leave. I started to scoot back to shove my chair away from the table, but I saw Callie's face. Her eyes narrowed and her mouth tightened. She wasn't going anywhere. The last thing Callie wanted to do was look weak or scared in front of the older girls. If she was brave enough to do this, I was too.

"Good!" Violet clapped her hands. "Looks like you're all in."

"What will we have to do?" Heather asked, maintaining her half bored, half mildly interested tone.

"You'll find out soon," Violet said. "Tomorrow, we'll send you a message telling you when and where to meet us next."

We nodded. I just wanted to get out of here! The room was freezing and creepy and if *one* spider even dangled near me . . .

"Tomorrow then," Georgia said. "You can leave now."

Without a word, we shuffled out of the room and left the Belles inside. Callie pulled the door shut behind us and I swear I heard the Belles laughing.

14

MY NEW BFF

MR. CONNER'S CLINIC, DAY 5
DAYS WITH ZERO CONTACT FROM JACOB:
I STOPPED COUNTING.

TAP! TAP!

What was that? I raised my head off my pillow and looked at the clock. 5:55 a.m. on a Friday. No one would knock on my door at—

Bang!

I threw my feet over the side of the bed and hurried to the door. I pulled it open and saw Brianna. Even at this early hour, she looked perfectly put together in slouch boots, black tights, a cream and sage green checkered mini and a matching green sweater. She eyed my frog-wearing-a-tiara pajamas and smirked.

"Cute," she said. "I should have worn my stars-and-moon pair."

I blushed. "Did you want to come in?"

"No, thanks. I've got other stops to make. Here." She handed me an ivory-colored envelope.

"But . . . ?"

Brianna turned and walked off.

I ripped the envelope open and pulled out a card with plum-colored shiny lacquered edges. The text gleamed in foiled gold.

> **Please join Violet, Brianna, and Georgia**
> **in front of the stables at midnight on**
> **Wednesday. Do not show this to anyone.**
> **—V, B, & G**

I reread the card, but still couldn't find any clues about initiation. Sigh. I could decide *not* to go, but then I'd be the only one. Heather didn't want to go either, I could tell, but she'd at least show up to save face. Now I had six days to worry about it.

I put the card on my desk and checked my riding schedule. I had a session with Mr. Bright in a couple of hours. He'd probably ask questions about the section of the handbook I'd forgotten to study last night.

I texted Eric. *Going 2 the caf 2 study handbook 4 half an hr. Want 2 come?*

He texted back right away. *Time?*

I desperately needed a shower first. *30 mins?*

C u then.

Twenty-five minutes later, I emerged from Winchester smelling like my new dark chocolate body wash and vanilla shampoo. I tucked my handbook under my arm and got a bowl of Frosted Flakes. Most of the cafeteria was shut down since many of the students were home on break. It was weird to only see one lunch lady and dozens of empty tables.

I sat at a table in the center of the caf and started paging through my handbook. Eric came in a few seconds later. He piled his tray with cantaloupe, eggs, and a blueberry bagel before coming over and sitting across from me. His hair was messy and he yawned as he took his seat.

"I didn't wake you up, did I?" I asked. "I forgot that it was so early."

Eric smiled. "It's okay. I needed to get up anyway."

"I'm so sorry! I'll make sure it's semilight out before I text next time."

He waved me away casually. "What're we studying?"

I shifted the book so he could see. "Natural ways to calm horses."

"Things I know *so* much about already," Eric teased.

"Me too. Eat, then read?" I suggested.

"Sure." We dug into our food and chatted while we ate. A couple of riders from other schools came in and spread out among the tables.

When we finished, Eric took our trays and I opened the handbook to chapter five. Eric grabbed a pen for notes and I started reading. We worked fast to make it to the end of the chapter and then took turns quizzing each other.

"Maybe we should light a few aromatherapy candles before a show," Eric said.

"Yeah! Like carrot, sugar, and peppermint scents?" I asked.

"Exactly. Who doesn't love the smell of hot carrots in the air?"

I closed the book and checked my watch. "I've got to get going. See you around the stable?"

"See you later."

We smiled at each other and I got up and headed for the door.

"Don't try to patent my genius candle idea without me!" Eric called after me.

15
STRESS BUSTER
FOR CHARM

INSIDE THE STABLE, I CAME AROUND THE corner and saw Jasmine leaning her back against Charm's stall door. She had her arms crossed over her chest and her eyes followed me as I walked up the aisle. *She* should have been named Phoenix. She kept disappearing and then popping back up again.

"Why are you standing near my horse?" I asked, looking inside to be sure he was okay.

"Oooh, so protective," Jasmine said. "Relax. I didn't even look at your nag. I came to talk to you."

I stepped closer to her. "I told you *never* to call him that."

Jasmine lowered her eyes for a second and then raised her chin. "Whatever. I only came to find out why you bother."

"Bother with what?" I asked impatiently. I so didn't have time for her games today.

"Coming to the clinic. You keep messing up. The teachers are probably laughing about you behind your back. You're the worst rider here. The lunging? I was embarrassed *for* you."

I took a deep breath. "I don't have time for this," I said. "We have class. And get used to it—I'm here whether you like it or not."

"Fine," Jasmine said. She pulled out a clear, shiny gloss and smoothed it over her lips. "Till they kick you out."

I glared at her and saw Callie standing just behind Jasmine. I wondered how long she'd been there. Her mouth was open, as if she wanted to say something. Had she come to defend me against Jasmine? Callie's eyes met mine and I knew it—she wanted to tell Jas to go fall in a muck pile. But she wouldn't because of the Eric sitch.

Finally, Jasmine, and then Callie, walked away. I reached for the sliding bolt on Charm's stall door and stepped into the stall. After a quick grooming, Charm and I headed for the indoor arena. My schedule had said to bring Charm untacked. I crossed my fingers that it wouldn't be lunging again.

When everyone in my group arrived, Mr. Bright stepped

into the center of the arena. "Hi, everyone," he said. "You ready to get started?"

We nodded.

"Today, we're going to work on stretching our horses. We'll also talk about techniques to calm an anxious horse. Go ahead and spread out around the arena and keep your horses facing me."

We did as he asked. Charm and I ended up between Violet and Cole.

Charm kept an eye on Phoenix—his new rival—and I took a breath. This had to go well—no matter what.

The arena door opened and Eric led a dark bay mare inside. It was Hazel—one of Mr. Conner's lesson horses. Eric handed the mare's lead line to Mr. Bright and gave me a quick smile on his way out.

"This is Hazel," Mr. Bright said. "She's my assistant for this session. You'll watch me demonstrate with Hazel before you try it with your horse. If you need help, I'll be right over. Let's get started."

We all kept our eyes on Mr. Bright and Hazel.

"Does anyone have a horse with a previous or current leg injury?" Mr. Bright asked.

We shook our heads. "Good," he said. "Now watch as I stretch Hazel's foreleg."

Mr. Bright ran his hand down Hazel's left front leg and asked her to lift it. He stood in front of her and took his time bringing her leg forward. We watched as he stretched the other legs and told us to try. After half an hour of leg stretching, Mr. Bright taught us signs of a stressed horse. Charm slept through most of the discussion—like he needed stress relief.

"That's it for today's exercises," Mr. Bright said at the end of the class. "Before you go, I'm going to ask each of you a question from last night's reading. After you've answered correctly, you may leave. If you miss your question, you have to stay while I ask the rest of the students theirs. Then, I'll ask you another."

"Jasmine," Mr. Bright said. "What's the purpose of blindfolding a horse?"

Jasmine froze. "Umm, you blindfold to . . . help the horse go to sleep?"

Mr. Bright gave her a sympathetic smile. "No. Stay there. Let me ask that question to Aaron."

"Horses feel safe blindfolded because they can't see whatever they thought was dangerous," Aaron said. "So, they have to follow whoever is leading them."

"Great, Aaron. See you next class," Mr. Bright said.

Aaron nodded and led his horse out of the arena.

"Sasha, if Charm got nervous before a show, how would you calm him?" Mr. Bright asked.

I didn't need the handbook to teach me that. "I'd lead him in small circles, talk to him and take him away from the busyness of the event."

"Good ideas," he said. "You may go."

I patted Charm's neck and led him out of the arena. I had a feeling Jasmine would be there for a while.

16

THE BOY-STEALERS
DESERVE EACH OTHER

BY THE TIME I'D GOTTEN CHARM BACK TO HIS stall, I was in full-out daydream mode. I couldn't stop obsessing about the e-mail. It had been three days. Three. Days. Jacob totally had to have read it by now. What, he couldn't e-mail back to say *anything*? This was torture! Had I gone too far by telling him I liked him? It had felt like the right thing to do at the time, but maybe it just totally freaked him out. Maybe I should have just stopped at the apology. Or maybe I—

Charm snorted and jerked me out of my fog. "What?" I asked him. Then I saw it. "Oh, Charm! I'm sorry!"

I'd accidentally put grain in his water bucket. I threw everything out and started over. Charm rubbed his head up and down on my arm like he was trying to remove his halter.

"Poor boy," I said. "I'm the worst." His halter was inside out. I fixed it and looked at him. "Do you want to go outside? I'll get you a blanket and you can hang out in the pasture for a while."

Charm nodded.

I grabbed his blue quilted blanket from the tack room and buckled him into it, making sure it was snug before I led him outside.

"You can stay out while I clean your tack," I said. "Then I'll bring you in."

Charm's breath was visible in the cold air as he followed me to the pasture. I saw another horse grazing in the side field. Charm saw the horse, too. His pace quickened and he let out a loud neigh.

The horse's head jerked up and turned in our direction. Now I could see it was Black Jack. Charm practically pulled me to the gate, his breath steaming out of his nostrils.

"Easy," I said, giving his lead line a little tug. Charm shifted from hoof to hoof as I unlatched the gate.

"I guess this has been tough on you," I said, nodding toward Black Jack, Charm's best buddy.

My frozen fingers fumbled as I tried to unclip the lead line from his halter. "Go have fun." I snapped the clip off

Charm's halter and he bolted forward. Black Jack, in a red blanket, tore off at a fast canter from the far end of the pasture.

I closed the gate and climbed the fence to watch them. Across the pasture, Callie stood on the lowest board of the fence. Our eyes met before we both turned back quickly to watch the horses. Their hooves pounded the ground as they stretched into gallops. My breath caught. For a second, I thought they'd collide. But they slid to a halt inches before banging heads. They touched noses and their visible breaths mingled and floated into the sky.

I couldn't take my eyes off them. Having fun together. I looked at Callie again. Things were a mess.

Charm playfully nipped Black Jack's neck and Jack shot off at a canter to the opposite end of the field. Charm took off after him and the horses seemed to play tag. Their red and blue blankets were vibrant against the dry winter grass. When Charm reached Jack, the dark horse turned around and chased Charm. They thundered down the pasture as they galloped up and down the fence line. Then, as quickly as they'd started their game, they stopped and started to graze.

I took a deep, calming breath and smoothed on my

stress-fighting eucalyptus gloss. It was time to say something to Callie. She needed to understand about Eric. I hopped down from the fence and walked toward her.

Callie, I practiced in my head. *Please listen to me and really believe that Eric and I are just* friends. *I still like Jacob.*

I was yards away when her phone rang. She pulled it out of her pocket.

"Hey!" she said. "What're you doing?"

I stopped. She wasn't even paying attention to me. It was all about the Mystery Caller.

"The clinic is going really well," she said.

She looked over and saw me. "Hold on," she said into the phone and turned to me. "Problem?" she asked, tucking a lock of black hair away from her face.

I could have screamed. Our horses were smarter and more mature than we were!

"Never mind," I said. I turned and headed back to the stable. Callie knew where to find me if she ever wanted to talk. But that didn't seem likely.

Inside the toasty tack room, I filled a small bucket with warm water and grabbed a tin of saddle soap. I folded a saddle pad on an overturned bucket and sat down by Charm's saddle. I took off the stirrup leathers and mixed my sponge into the water and soap. I started scrubbing as

hard as I could. The yellow soap bubbled on the leather and I splattered soapy water onto the floor. I brushed hair out of my eyes and cleaned the seat with both hands.

"Are you *trying* to ruin your saddle?"

I looked up at Julia and Alison, standing in the doorway. They closed the door and stared at me.

"Did you come to clean tack, too?" I asked.

"Hardly," Julia said. "We *saw* you."

I looked up at her. "Okay . . ."

"With Callie," Alison finished. "Stop trying to make her your friend again. She doesn't want to talk to you."

"Stay out of it," I said. "Callie and I *will* become friends again sooner or later, so you need to get over it."

Julia laughed. "Whatever. And you can have your new BFF Heather. You two boy-stealers deserve each other."

Callie totally had to stop telling people that I "stole" Eric!

"Yeah," Alison said. "And you can tell your new best friend that we're not talking to her till she dumps Ben and apologizes to Julia. Maybe we'll *never* talk to her."

They opened the door, exited, and then slammed it behind them.

Callie used to hate Julia and Alison and now she was hanging out with them more than she hung out with

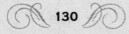

me. I couldn't believe her! Plus, no matter what Callie thought I did, she didn't have to blab our private business to people who already hated me. She was taking this too far. Part of me—gag—felt sorry for Julia. Her BFF had stolen her BF. I didn't know how that felt, but I could imagine it was completely awful.

Once I finished scrubbing Charm's tack, I put it away and went out to the pasture to get him. Black Jack was already gone. Charm nudged me with his muzzle and practically pranced back to the stable.

"Feeling good, huh?" I asked him. "You needed to hang out with Jack. Just like I still want to be friends with Callie."

He stood still while I took off his blanket. As soon as I was done, he ambled to the quietest corner of his stall and started to fall asleep.

"Sasha?" Mike came up behind me. "Mr. Conner wants to see you in his office."

"Just me?" I asked, wondering what I'd done wrong. Had he heard how awful I was during the lunging exercise?

"No, you and the other seventh-grade advanced team."

"Oh. Okay, thanks."

I left Charm and went to Mr. Conner's office. Julia, Alison, and Callie—aka the Trio II—were already waiting inside. I grabbed a seat in the front and Heather came inside and sat by me.

Mr. Conner walked in and shut the door. "We need to have a serious talk," he said.

Uh-oh.

"I take that back. *I'll* talk, you'll listen," he said. He stood with his arms crossed in front of him, looking down at us. It suddenly occurred to me that a back row seat would have been a better idea.

"Over the past few days, I've noticed several things. Distraction, fighting, ignoring, glaring. Am I right?"

No one moved.

Mr. Conner unfolded his arms to gesture. "Look at yourselves. You're supposed to be a *team*. This is not how my advanced team members act. The behavior all of you have displayed during the clinic has been below Canterwood's—and my—standards. It will *not* continue. Understood?"

We nodded.

"You will start acting like a team or this will be the last invite to a clinic that you'll receive. Scouts and trainers value teamwork. If you don't start acting like a team, others will take notice . . . if they haven't already." He paused. I kept my eyes down, and out of the corners of

my eyes, I saw that Heather's head was bent, too. "You may leave."

We stood and left the office silently. Callie, Julia, and Alison veered down the main aisle and Heather and I ended up going for the side door. We almost smacked into Jasmine. She'd probably been lurking to try to hear what Mr. Conner had said to us.

"Watch it!" Jasmine snipped. She looked at us and smiled. "You two! Together again. That's just sad, Heather. Did you lose all of your real friends?"

"Aw, you're just upset that we can totally take you in the arena," Heather said. "Is the clinic just too much for you, Jas?"

Jasmine laughed and adjusted her leather gloves. "You wish. I'm just sorry that Sasha's the best you can do for a friend. But don't worry. You'll have better options soon."

Jasmine stepped around us and walked away.

"What did *that* mean?" I asked.

"I have no idea," Heather said. "And I really don't care."

We zipped up our coats and stepped outside, ambling toward the courtyard. "We're getting distracted from the real issue, aren't we?" I asked.

Heather suddenly slowed. "We can't get yelled at like that again. Mr. Conner will kick us out next time."

"It's been hard to focus," I admitted. "The thing with Callie is messing with me."

I expected Heather to laugh or make a snarky comment, but instead she looked at me and nodded.

"I get that, but you have to remember why we're here. To ride. This is our big chance in front of the scouts. Look, I'm not your biggest fan . . ." I rolled my eyes. "But you're not a bad rider."

I stopped. "Say that again? I thought I heard you say I'm not a bad rider."

Heather snorted. "I'll deny I ever said that. But it's kind of true. You're not the best rider here, but you work harder than a lot of people. Like Julia and Alison."

"But they're so good that they don't have to work as hard," I said.

Heather shook her head. "No way. When you get that 'good,' you have to work harder to stay there. They don't realize that."

I almost forgot I was talking to Heather. This felt like a conversation I could have with Callie.

"So . . . how do we get our focus back?" I asked.

"I don't care how you fix your mess, but after this thing with the Belles on Wednesday night, I'm out. Done. Completely focusing on riding till after the demo."

"What about Ben?"

"I'm breaking up with him."

"After *all* of the fighting with Julia and Alison, you're *dumping* him?!"

We reached the stone benches in the courtyard and Heather perched at the edge of a bench.

I sat across from her. I'd never seen her like this—she looked like she wanted to cry.

"Ben was a stupid decision," Heather said. "Julia's one of my best friends. I knew she'd hate me and I did it anyway."

"Why?" I asked cautiously. "You can have any guy in our grade. Why go after *Julia's* boyfriend?"

I braced myself—expecting her to snap and morph back into normal Heather.

"Whatever, Sasha. Don't think I don't know what Canterwood boys think of me. They think I'm snobby and mean. Guys don't like me the way Jacob liked you."

"That's not true," I argued.

"Yes," Heather said. "It is."

I tried not to shake my head in disbelief. I never knew Heather had boy problems. She was pretty, smart, and a good rider. But I could see it in her face. She was afraid guys would reject her if they got to know the real

Heather—not the snarky, tough-girl front she showed most people.

"Then you should let them get to know you. You can be cool when you want to be. Not," I added, "that I ever said that."

Heather sniffed and let out a breath. "Thanks. I might actually consider your lame idea. But don't *ever* pep talk me again."

"Deal." I laughed.

17

RACE YOU!

MR. CONNER'S CLINIC, DAY 7
DAYS UNTIL BELLES MEETING: 4

IT WAS LATE ON SUNDAY MORNING AND I HAD the day off from classes. I had just gotten off the phone with my parents and had worked hard to sound cheerful and not at all stressed. Mom had wanted to talk more about the clinic, but when I'd told her I had to go work Charm, she'd let me go.

Charm *did* need a workout, but I didn't want to practice. What had happened to riding for fun? I missed trail riding and exploring the woods around the campus.

I pulled on my riding boots. *You and Charm both need the practice, so stop whining,* I told myself.

I checked my e-mail one last time. *Zero unread messages.*

Argh!!!! I was *so* sick of seeing that message! Maybe my e-mail to Jacob had gotten lost. But if I re-sent it and he got it twice, I'd look desperate. I shut down the computer and looked at my phone. I didn't *have* to ride for practice. If I wanted to trail ride, why not?

Trail ride in a few mins. Want 2 go? I sent the message to Eric.

Last 1 tacked up has 2 buy hot choc.

I smiled, yanked on black paddock boots and a coat and hurried to the mirror. I quickly twisted my hair into a bed-head, I-didn't-take-forever-to-do-this ponytail and pulled a few tendrils around my face.

I jogged to the stable. Eric wasn't in Luna's stall, so I figured I had him beat. I ran to the tack room, hoping Mr. Conner wouldn't catch me sprinting, and saw Eric inside. His back was to me—he was gathering Luna's tack into his arms.

"You!" I said. "You're not going to win."

"Ha!" Eric teased, spinning around. "I'm already out the door. Bye!"

"This *so* isn't over!" I huffed, racing over to Charm's saddle rack.

He skirted around me and ran out. I noticed that Phoenix's tack was missing from the rack next to Charm's and figured Jasmine had probably paid Mike or Doug to clean it. I scooped Charm's gleaming saddle and bridle into my arms and hurried to his stall.

"Charm," I said, hurriedly. "Want to trail ride?"

Charm pricked his ears at my voice and stepped up to the stall door. He nickered at me and stood back to let me open the door. As I crosstied him, Eric brushed Luna on a set of crossties ahead of me.

"You're behind, Silver," Eric called.

"Keep telling yourself that, Rodriguez," I said.

I picked Charm's hooves and whisked a body brush over him. Charm *knew* it was a race. His ears pointed forward and he struck the ground with his left foreleg. He stood still while I saddled him and opened his mouth easily to take the bit.

"Almost done!" I taunted.

"Too late!" Eric said.

We unclipped our horses at the same time and I led Charm toward Eric and Luna.

Eric was a few steps ahead of me. *He's going to win!* Then I saw his helmet on the counter.

"Not so fast," I said. "You forgot something."

Eric looked over his shoulder, but kept walking. "Oh, sure. I know your tricks. I didn't forget . . ." He reached up and felt his head. "Oh."

He circled Luna back and Charm and I passed him.

"Better get your wallet," I teased, giggling as Charm and I headed outside.

A few seconds later, Eric and Luna reached Charm and me. He shook his head and smiled. "You got me," he said. "I totally blew my lead."

"I'll take my hot chocolate with caramel, please," I informed him. I laughed so hard that my sides ached and tears spilled out of the corners of my eyes.

Eric shook his head. "Look at yourself," he said, but he was laughing too—almost as hard as I was.

I thought about how lucky I was that Eric had decided to stay. He was fast becoming my closest friend aside from Paige. The clinic would have been totally miserable without him. He made the bad stuff going on with Jasmine and Callie seem less overwhelming. Plus, I always smiled the entire time I was with him.

We mounted our horses and turned Charm and Luna toward Blackwell. They stepped onto a dirt path that snaked behind the dorms, matching each others' strides.

The dark gray sky was filled with wispy clouds. I took a deep breath of crisp, cold air.

"I can't believe the clinic is almost halfway over," I said. "It's going by so fast."

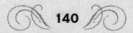

"I know," Eric said. "It feels like my parents just gave me permission to stay."

"They must be proud that you're such a good rider."

"They are," he said. "But my mom wasn't thrilled at first. She wanted me to do the typical guy sports like soccer or football because she thought I'd get teased. My dad told her I'd learn how to handle it if kids picked on me."

Luna snorted as a bird flew off the trail and under a pile of brush. Eric ran a hand down her neck. "Easy, girl," he said to her.

"Wow," I murmured. "I never thought about that. *Did* anyone ever tease you?"

Eric locked eyes with me for a second like he was debating whether or not to say something. "Yeah, they did."

"I'm sorry. You don't have to tell me."

"No, it's okay. I don't mind." He took a breath and rubbed his thumbs over the tops of the reins. "In fifth grade, I'd just started riding and my friends kept asking me why I wouldn't stay after school and join the baseball team with them. I told them I wanted to ride and they didn't get it. They started teasing me for doing a 'girly sport.'"

"That's *so* dumb. I'm sorry you had to deal with that." I almost reached over and squeezed his elbow, but I stopped

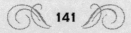

short. My relationship with Eric had gotten so confused by Callie—and everyone else—I hated that I couldn't do something as simple as comforting a friend for fear that someone would see and blow it out of proportion.

"It's okay," Eric continued. "But those guys wouldn't stop harassing me. When I got to my desk one morning, I found a message written on it."

"What did it say?"

Eric laughed. "It said, 'Go back to the barn and kiss your horse!' in red marker."

I clenched the reins with my fingers. "Those stupid boys! What did you do?"

"Nothing. Actually, the message itself was so lame, I didn't really care. But when my teacher saw it and asked me who did it, I wouldn't tell her. But the guys were afraid of being caught, so they messed with me and threatened me when teachers weren't around. That was the worst of it."

The trail took a sharp turn, twisting along a semifrozen creek bank. We eased the horses to a slow walk and guided them carefully along the bank. I was furious to think that those jerks had teased Eric.

"Did it ever stop?" I asked.

"For the most part. But one of these guys pretty much

teased me until the day I left," Eric said. "At Canterwood, it's okay that I'm a guy *and* a rider. The equestrian team is so prestigious, no one cares if I go to soccer practice on Tuesday and ride on Wednesday. Plus, there are other guy riders here."

"Yeah, well, they shouldn't have cared at your old school either. Girls *and* guys can ride. But you'll show them. When you make it big, they'll be jealous."

Eric smiled. "You're a good friend to say so."

We edged the horses along the creek and into a thicker spot of woods. The horses' hooves were muffled along the dirt path and Charm drifted closer to Luna. Eric and I guided the horses around a fallen tree that blocked half of the trail. We approached a low-hanging branch and ducked as Charm and Luna walked under it.

"Do you know what you want to do when you're older?" I asked. "Anything with horses?"

"I want to open a training stable one day. Maybe give lessons like Mr. Conner."

"That's so cool!" I edged Charm closer to Luna. "A training stable would be amazing. You'd get to work with so many different horses and learn how to handle all of their personalities."

"Exactly. What about you?"

I shook my head.

"Tell me. What?" Eric's eyes seemed to smile at me.

"Well . . . I know it will never happen, but I want to ride on the United States Equestrian Team and compete in the Olympics. And, while I'm trying to qualify, I want to open my own stable."

"That's great! And the reason it would 'never happen' would be . . . what?"

"It's almost *impossible* to get on the team. Out of the thousands of riders who are good enough, only a few make it. That's why I want to open a stable too—as backup."

"Sasha, you *are* good enough," Eric said. "You'll be perfect for them."

"Thanks." I grinned. "There's a lot of work to do between now and then. Making the Youth Equestrian National Team would be a big step."

"That's why this clinic is so important. It's your shot to impress scouts," Eric said.

I nodded, letting the words sink in. Eric was right. If I wanted to ride in the Olympics, this was my first big chance to impress important people. Everything else— Jacob, the Belles, and Callie—had to come second. I had to find a way to focus on myself and worry less about situations I couldn't control.

"I should be more focused," I said. "But it's been hard. I'm fighting with Callie, and she was my best friend."

"Have you tried talking to her?"

"Only a thousand times." I dropped the reins over Charm's neck and reached my hands to the sky. "She won't listen. And it's so stupid. It's all because of—" I stopped and shook my head. "It's just stupid."

"Because of what?" Eric asked. "What were you going to say?"

I sighed. Eric was my friend—I could talk to him. Nothing I said could make this situation worse. "Because of you."

Eric gently pulled Luna to a halt and I stopped Charm beside her. "*Me?* Why?!"

"Well . . ." I paused and swallowed. "Callie really liked you, but then she kept seeing us together, and she thought I stole you from her. It's crazy because I told her I liked Jacob, and that you and I were just friends, but she wouldn't believe me and now she hates me for no reason!" Phew! Felt good to say that. And now that it was out, I felt silly for not saying anything to Eric sooner.

"Oh," Eric said. "Wow. I had no idea that Callie liked me. Is there anything I can do to help?"

I thought for a minute. If I could get Eric and Callie together . . .

"Do you like Callie?"

Eric hesitated. "She seems nice—I mean, aside from the whole ignoring-my-friend Sasha thing."

"She is nice! She's so friendly and smart. Plus, she's the best rider I've ever met. I'll give you her cell number and you can text her sometime. If you want."

Eric handed me his phone. "It might help you get your friendship back, huh?"

I nodded as I punched in the number. "I think so. Then, she'd definitely believe me."

I handed him back the phone. This plan couldn't fail. Eric and Callie would start dating, Callie would forgive me, and if Jacob would ever e-mail me, I'd get him back, too!

"Want to trot out of the woods and canter through that field?" Eric asked.

"Let's go!"

18

I H8 SPAM

BACK AT WINCHESTER, I LOGGED IN TO ICHAT.
I'd texted Paige on the walk back from my ride with Eric
and she'd been free to meet me online. After our trail ride,
Eric and I had agreed to text later and set up a study time
for tonight.

"Hellooo!" Paige said, when she saw me. She leaned
closer to the screen and covered her mouth. "OMG, you
made up with Jacob!"

"What?"

"Your face! You're all pink and you look sooo happy!
Tell me, tell me!"

"Paige!" I said, holding up my hands in a wait-a-sec
gesture. "I didn't make up with Jacob. I haven't even talked
to him yet!"

Paige slumped backward. "Really? I'm so sorry—you just haven't looked this happy in a while and I thought it was because of Jacob. Did you make up with Callie?"

"Not yet—but I think I will soon. I just got back from a trail ride with Eric. I gave him Callie's number and he said he's going to call her. I figure if Callie sees I'm not with Eric, we can be friends again."

"Hmmm . . . ," Paige straightened her broad white satin headband. "That might work. And Eric doesn't like anyone else?"

"I don't think so . . . at least he's never said a word to me about it."

"Let me know what happens. I really miss being there!"

I rolled my eyes. "Paige, you're on the set of a TV show. You can't seriously miss school!"

"I do!" she said. "I know I'm a total dork, but I'm ready to get back to classes and see my friends. The set is great and it's nice to visit Mom and Dad, but I'm ready to come back."

"Paige!" a voice said behind her.

"Hold on, Mom!" Paige turned toward her door. "Be right there!" She looked back at me. "Gotta go. Text me later."

"Bye." I closed out iChat and pulled up my e-mail.

Two unread messages.

!!!!!

Please be from Jacob. Pleeeeeaaaase be from Jacob. I opened my inbox and scanned the senders. Spam. Both spam. Sigh.

"I'm *not* going to miss Jacob," I said out loud. "I'm not."

But I did. He was never going to e-mail me. Ever. I flopped onto my bed and sighed. Boys were the worst.

My text alert chimed. It was Eric. *Study @ 7?*

Most def!

I smiled and thought about how nice our trail ride had been earlier. Soon, all thoughts of the Jacob drama had vanished and I was thinking about my friend and how much fun we always had together. Eric was a good person, and I was lucky to have him in my life.

19

TRADING FRIENDS
FOR GUYS

MR. CONNER'S CLINIC, DAY 8
DAYS LEFT TILL BELLES MEETING: 3

"PAY ATTENTION, COLE! VIOLET, WATCH YOUR hands!" Miss Cho called.

It was Monday morning and she'd been tough on us for the whole lesson. At least today's focus wasn't dressage. Miss Cho had decided to let us do flatwork for the day. Charm and I hadn't messed up *once*. We were both in good moods.

"Sit deep and urge your horses forward with your legs," Miss Cho said. We'd been doing a sitting trot for a couple of laps and Charm's gait was even.

"Sasha," Miss Cho said.

I looked over at her nervously. "Yes?"

"Charm looks excellent. As do you. Nice work."

I grinned and Jasmine turned around to glare at me.

"Slow your horses to a walk," Miss Cho said. "I need to grab Mike and then we'll begin a new exercise."

We followed her instructions.

"Congrats, Sasha," Jasmine said. "You're able to control Charm's walk. Score!"

"Thanks, Jas!" I said. "I mastered the walk after seeing how you couldn't control Phoenix's trot. Thanks for the inspiration."

Miss Cho stepped out of the arena and returned a couple of minutes later with Mike.

They went to the back of the arena and picked up white cavalletti from the ground. Miss Cho and Mike worked together and set up four cavalletti, or portable jumps, that were often only a couple of inches high, down the center of the arena. The poles were held with wooden Xs at the ends.

"We're going to take the horses over the cavalletti that have been spaced enough to encourage your horses to lengthen their strides," Miss Cho said. "We're not trying to get your horse to jump, but rather to trot over these poles and pay attention to their hoof placement."

I stroked Charm's neck and straightened my helmet as I listened.

"Keep a safe distance between yourself and the other

riders. Go ahead and trot to the end of the arena, turn back and then walk over the cavalletti."

"Walk?" Jasmine questioned, sounding bored.

"Yes, walk," Miss Cho said. She gave Jasmine the say-another-word-and-you're-in-trouble look. "Does anyone know why we're walking first?"

Aaron raised his hand and Miss Cho nodded to him.

"You want to be sure the horse can walk over the cavalletti first without hitting them. If not, then you're probably not ready to trot without lowering them or walking through a few more times."

"Yes," Miss Cho said. "Exactly. Let's begin."

I asked Charm to trot and we squeezed behind Violet. Aaron, Cole and Jasmine lined up after me and we trotted down the center of the arena, bypassing the cavalletti. Charm and I had worked over cavalletti a lot back home in Union, so I wasn't worried.

I turned Charm to face the poles and slowed him to a walk.

"Be sure to give him rein, Sasha, and let him look at the poles," Miss Cho said.

Charm lowered his head and looked at the cavalletti. He seemed to think about where he placed each hoof and made it through without nicking a pole.

"Good boy," I said, patting his neck. He stepped to the side of the arena and we waited for everyone else to go.

"Let's do them one more time at a walk," Miss Cho said, once everyone had finished their rides.

Jasmine rolled her eyes when Miss Cho wasn't looking. We walked over the cavalletti and Miss Cho raised the first pole a couple of inches.

"We'll go through it again and keep raising one pole at a time until all of the cavalletti are the same height as the first pole," she said.

Charm and I reached the cavalletti first and he stepped over them without a second glance. Everyone repeated the process until all of the poles were raised.

"Let's trot through them now," Miss Cho said.

Charm and I started for the cavalletti, but Jasmine weaved Phoenix around us and cut Charm off. She angled Phoenix at the cavalletti and kicked him into a fast trot.

"Jasmine!" Miss Cho called. "Slow down!"

Jasmine acted as if she didn't hear. Phoenix tried to lower his head to look at the poles, but Jasmine tugged it up and heeled him forward. Phoenix tripped on the first cavalletti and didn't have time to recover. He knocked over the second pole and clipped the third. With a strong effort, he managed to clear the fourth. None of that was

his fault, but Jasmine acted as if it was. She yanked him around in a circle and pulled him to a halt.

"Ms. King, dismount *now*," Miss Cho's voice was hard. "Lead your horse out of the arena, cool him, and groom him. Then, go to Mr. Conner's office. Tell him you're waiting for me."

Jasmine didn't even argue. She hopped off Phoenix and led him out of the arena. Miss Cho shook her head and took a breath.

"Please continue at a trot," she told us.

"Go ahead," Violet said. She motioned for me to go in front of her.

I eased Charm forward and made sure he didn't trot too fast. He snapped his knees up over the poles and glided over them.

Violet, Cole, and Aaron did the same. I was relieved that none of us had given the already upset Miss Cho one more reason to get mad at us.

"Once more and we're finished," Miss Cho said. "You're all doing great."

She watched us ride over the cavalletti again—not one horse ticked a rail.

"Excellent." Miss Cho smiled. "Thank you. I'll see you at the next class."

As I led Charm out of the arena, Heather and Aristocrat came in from the outdoor arena. She looked behind me, watching Cole, Aaron, and Violet leave the arena. "Where's Jasmine?" she asked.

"She got kicked out," I said. "It was awful. She rushed Phoenix over cavalletti and didn't listen when Miss Cho told her to stop. She's waiting for Miss Cho in Mr. Conner's office."

Heather grinned. "I feel bad for Phoenix, but not for Jasmine. The instructors needed to see what kind of rider she really is."

"No kidding. I can't wait for her to just go back to Wellington already." *Callie would have loved this,* I thought. She'd disliked Jasmine ever since Jas had harassed me at the Junior Equestrian Regionals. I frowned.

Heather looked at me and slowed Aristocrat. "Thinking about Callie?"

"Maybe," I said with a shrug. "I just wish we could *all* stop fighting."

I stopped Charm by his stall and Heather led Aristocrat forward. "This hurts me to say, but we're more alike than I thought," Heather said.

"What? How?"

"We both chose to give up our friends for guys we

weren't supposed to have." Heather turned and walked off.

"I don't 'have' Eric!" I called after her. "For the millionth time, we're *just friends*!"

But Heather was already gone.

20

THANKS,
BUT NO

I WALKED ACROSS THE CAF TO AN EMPTY TABLE. Along the way, my stomach growled so loud, I looked around to see if anyone else heard it. But no one was looking at me. Phew. I slid into my seat and tried not to stuff my face with fries.

"Hungry, huh?" Eric asked, taking a seat across from me.

I nodded. "I can't believe it's already Tuesday," I said. "The demo's on Saturday!"

"I know. I can't wait to watch you ride." He took a giant bite of his turkey and lettuce sub.

"Did you hear anything about what happened to

Jasmine, by the way? I left before I could find out what happened."

Eric put down his sandwich. "She got suspended from today's classes. She has to watch from the side."

"Oooh, man. She's going to be *ma-ad* today!"

"You should have seen her leave Mr. Conner's office," Eric said. "Her face was beet red and she stomped away so hard, I'm surprised her boot heels didn't break off."

We laughed and I looked around to be sure Jasmine wasn't lurking to spill something on me again. But luckily, she was never in the cafeteria—and today was no exception.

"Oh! Did you text Callie yet?" I asked. "I'm dying for you to ask her out. She'll be so excited!"

"Actually . . . ," Eric started. He looked at his lap.

"What? You haven't texted her yet?"

"No, I did. But she said no."

I stared at him. *"What?"*

"She said thanks, but no." Eric shrugged.

"Ohmigod! What is wrong with her?! She's wanted to go out with you for forever. Text her again. She must just been surprised or maybe—"

"Sash, it's okay. Really. She said no. It's no big deal."

Why wasn't he more upset about this? I folded my

arms on the table and banged my head against them. "It *is* a big deal. This was supposed to prove to Callie that I never betrayed her."

"I'm sure you'll find another way," Eric said.

"Unless . . . ," Maybe Callie didn't care about Eric because she was back to the old Callie! The all-boys-annoy-me Callie. Maybe she'd just needed time. Maybe she'd even listen to me now.

Eric looked at me suspiciously. "Uh-oh. You already thought of another way, didn't you?"

I smiled. He knew me too well.

"Now that you're done setting me up," Eric teased. "Want to study?"

"Sure." I pulled out my handbook and we got to work.

21

MY EX-BFF
HAS A BF

CHARM AND I HEADED TO JUMPING CLASS WITH
Ms. Thorne. I'd looked around for Callie while grooming
and tacking up Charm, but hadn't seen her.

Violet and I were the first ones in the arena. We
mounted our horses and started to warm them up.

"Ready for tomorrow?" Violet asked, adjusting the
collar of her pretty, royal blue mockneck bell coat. I'd
never get away with a nice coat like that around Charm!
He'd sneeze, drool, or snort on me and my clothes would
be ruined.

"I'm ready," I said.

Jasmine walked into the arena and leaned against the
wall.

Cole and Aaron led their horses inside and Ms. Thorne

walked in right after them. Ms. Thorne had a look on her face that made me shiver. Today was going to be tough.

"Are all of your horses warmed up?" she asked.

"Yes," we told her in unison.

"Good. We're going to be jumping a few low verticals . . ."

Easy.

". . . without stirrups," Ms. Thorne continued.

Never mind.

"Go ahead and cross your stirrups over the pommel and sit deep in your saddle."

This was going to be painful. I sighed and waited for my turn. This time, I would *not* obsess about the e-mail—or Callie. I would stay focused. Charm and I had to do better.

Forty-five minutes later, I pulled Charm to a trot as we finished our final ride.

"Best ride of the class, Sasha," Ms. Thorne said. "Maybe you should ride without stirrups from now on."

Everyone except Jasmine laughed. Charm and I'd had a great ride—one of the best in days! That's how we needed to perform from now on. I patted Charm's neck and Ms. Thorne dismissed the class. I led Charm out of the arena and walked to cool him down.

I looked for Eric—I had to tell him about my ride!

But he wasn't in the aisles. I hurried to untack and groom Charm.

"You were sooo good today, boy," I said. I put him in his stall and kissed his muzzle. "Love you."

Charm sniffed my hair for a second and then moved over to his hay net.

I gathered Charm's tack and carried it to the tack room.

". . . she thinks we don't know about her boyfriend . . ."

I stopped outside the door and peeked inside. Julia and Alison were huddled together by the saddle racks.

"Seriously. Could Callie be more obvious with the texting? Do you know who he is?" Alison asked.

Callie. Had. A boyfriend. I stopped midbreath.

My supposed-to-be BFF had a BF and she didn't tell me!! I struggled not to drop Charm's saddle with my sweaty hands. *That's* why she said no to Eric. She'd been dating someone and I'd had no clue. She obviously didn't even think of herself as my friend anymore—otherwise, she would have told me. I slumped against the wall.

"No—but I'm going to find out who he is," Julia said. "Then we'll decide what to do."

"She'd probably spill if we asked her," Alison added.

Julia laughed. "Where's the fun in that?"

I shifted closer to the door. I wanted to burst in and tell them not to mess with Callie, but I knew they'd just deny that they were up to anything.

"I'll try to grab her phone," Alison said. "Once we know who he is, then we can decide how to use that info."

They laughed and I clenched the saddle leather with my fingers. Without Heather, Julia and Alison had stepped up their game.

Boots scuffed against the floor and I darted away from the door, dragging Charm's tack with me.

Callie could *not* trust them! I had to warn her that— no. No. Callie hadn't listened to me for weeks. *She* didn't want to be my friend. She'd chosen Julia and Alison as her new BFFs. She'd never believe me anyway.

After I was sure Julia and Alison were gone, I put Charm's tack away and left the stable. Even though I'd had a great ride, as I walked back to Winchester, I was completely obsessed with Callie and her secret boyfriend.

Why had Callie given me such a hard time about Eric if she'd already had a boyfriend? And, most important of all, who was he?

22

MY NUMBER-
ONE GUY

MR. CONNER'S CLINIC, DAY 10
HOURS UNTIL BELLES MEETING: 16

TODAY WAS THE DAY. WELL, TOMORROW, I
guess, since I wasn't meeting the Belles until midnight.

I knew the day would drag if I didn't stay busy, so I'd
been at Charm's stall by seven in the morning. It was only
eight now, and I'd already groomed every inch of him. I
rubbed my fingers over his soft blaze and inspected my
grooming job.

"Charm, you look *so* handsome," I told him. His coat
had a deep sheen and his blaze was blinding white.

He tilted his head and gave me a look that said, *like
that's news.*

I tacked him up and led him down the aisle. The stable

was super-quiet today. Most of the riders were just starting to arrive and the horses peeked sleepily over their stall doors.

A low rumble came from Charm's throat. I looked up to see Callie and Jack standing in front of us.

"Hey," I said cautiously.

"Hi," Callie said. I noticed that she had a coat of mascara on and sparkly pink lip gloss. Callie *never* wore makeup to the stable. Ever. This was boyfriend related.

"Listen," I said. "Can we talk sometime? I know——"

"Cal! C'mon!" Alison and Sunstruck stepped between me and Callie. She grabbed Callie's arm and pulled her away. "We've got to get to our lesson."

Callie turned back to me. "I've got to go," Callie said to me. She, Alison, Sunstruck, and Jack walked toward the indoor arena.

I stared after her. Jealousy rippled through me. Callie had a boyfriend and my almost-boyfriend Jacob wouldn't even e-mail me back. Plus, she had Julia and Alison—two new best friends who hung out with her every second. *At least you've got Eric*, I reminded myself. Otherwise, I'd be totally alone.

I led Charm outside. His tail whipped from side to side and he yanked his head up and down. The reins slipped through my gloved fingers and I tightened my grip.

He sulked through Miss Cho's entire dressage lesson. My mood didn't help, either. Miss Cho told me twice to pay attention, but I just couldn't focus. Julia and Alison's voices swirled in my head and I kept remembering how many times I'd seen Callie texting her mystery guy. Charm and I moved mechanically through the drills.

After dressage, I had a break. I avoided everyone and took Charm to the back of the stable while we waited for Mr. Bright's class to start. He was supposed to teach us about herbal supplements for winter feeding.

"Sasha?" Doug asked, walking up to me.

"Yeah?"

"Mr. Bright had to cancel classes today. He had to leave for a family emergency."

"Oh, no! What happened?"

"His daughter was practicing cross-country today and her horse refused a jump. He slid right into a solid log and she went over his head and broke her shoulder."

"Oh, my God. Is she okay?"

Doug nodded. "She'll be fine. But Mr. Bright wanted to see her."

"Of course," I said. "Thanks for telling me."

Doug nodded and walked away, probably to let the other students know.

Accidents happened, but it didn't make them any less scary. Poor Mr. Bright had probably freaked when he'd gotten that call. A vision flashed in front of me—Charm slamming into a log because I wasn't paying attention.

I leaned against Charm and sighed. "That can't happen to us, boy," I said. I couldn't keep losing focus. I'd been so busy sulking and fixating on my problems that I'd forgotten to look out for my number one guy—Charm. He didn't deserve that.

"Let's get you untacked and back in your stall so you can rest, boy," I said. "You get the rest of today off. We'll start practicing hard tomorrow for the demo. We'll work as long as it takes to be sure we're ready for scouts, okay?"

Charm winked at me. I led him down the aisle, feeling better than I had in days. I just wished it hadn't taken a serious spill to make me see what was really important.

23

HE WANTS TO BE WHAT?!

BACK AT WINCHESTER, I GEARED UP FOR A long night of studying. I threw on my royal blue leggings, fuzzy crème-colored socks, and a thermal knit top. I half dried my hair—just enough so I wouldn't be cold—and then curled up in front of the warm fireplace in the common room.

I opened up my handbook and a bag of Chex Mix and began to read a passage about poisonous pasture plants. It was just past noon—twelve hours left until I met the Belles.

I'd made it through thirty pages when my phone rang.

OMG . . . that ringtone!

!!!!

I swiped my phone off the coffee table and blinked at the screen. JACOB.

"Hi," I said, trying not to sound as nervous as I felt.

"Um, hey, Sasha," Jacob said. "Look . . ."

I could hear him breathing. My chest felt crushed. Would he hang up on me before I got to say—

"I'm sorry!" we both blurted out at the same time.

"Can I go first?" Jacob asked, laughing a little.

"Sure."

He took a breath. "I've been a total jerk to you. I knew how much Heather bothered you . . . and I totally should have talked about it to you. I handled everything all wrong at the Sweetheart Soirée. And I shouldn't have avoided you after that. I'm really sorry."

I let out the breath I'd been holding pretty much since the Soirée.

"I'm sorry, too," I said hurriedly. "*I* was wrong to believe Heather over you. I should have talked to you the second I started worrying about the whole Heather thing. It was horrible the way I yelled at you in front of everyone."

"It's both our faults," Jacob said.

"I know. But it shouldn't have happened."

"Well, I know we can't take it back." He paused. "But I don't want to be stuck on it forever."

"Me neither."

"I'm okay if you're okay." Jacob's tone lightened.

"I am now."

We both laughed nervous laughs.

"Phew," I said. "I'm glad *that's* over."

"Me too."

"Have you been offline this whole time?" I asked. "It took you forever to read my e-mail."

"E-mail? I didn't get one from you."

Um.

"You didn't? Are you sure?"

"Yeah, or I would have e-mailed you back. Let me check again. . . ."

I heard Jacob's computer whir to life as he checked his e-mail. OMG, if he never got my e-mail then that meant he was calling me on his own. He'd wanted to talk to me! We had a chance to get back together and start over. I hugged myself with my free arm. A log crackled in the fireplace and cast a spark up into the chimney.

"Nope, nothing," he said. "That's so weird."

"It's okay," I said. "I'm just glad you called."

Now he'd tell me he couldn't wait to see me . . .

"It was good to talk. I'm glad we can still be friends after everything."

"Yeah! I'm so happy we're . . ."

WAIT! Did he say *friends*?

". . . um, friends," I finished, hoping he'd correct me.

"I've got to go, but I'll see you around campus soon," Jacob said.

"Right," I mumbled. "Bye."

The line went dead and I stared at the phone. He'd said friends. And meant it.

OH.

MY.

GOD.

NO!

I buried my head in my hands.

The e-mail! It was still out there! The one where I told him everything about how sorry I was and how I still liked him. What if it just showed up in his inbox and he read it *after* he'd just told me he wanted to be "friends"?

"Great," I said aloud. "Just great." I flopped onto my back on the couch and covered my burning face with a pillow. So much for not worrying about the little things. But this wasn't little. That was *huge*. I moaned into the pillow and kept it over my face.

I was *not* going to do this. I pulled off the pillow and sat up. When Jacob came back to Canterwood after break, I'd track him down and we'd talk. Again. And again . . .

until he believed that I was sorry. He still liked me—I knew he did. He'd realize that once he saw me.

I smiled to myself. There. I had a plan and I would get him back. I could do this. But until then, I was all about the clinic. Jacob would be so proud when I told him how Charm and I had impressed the scouts.

I opened my handbook again and started to read. Eleven hours to go.

24

INITIATION

BUZZZZZ! I ROLLED OVER IN BED AND HIT THE off button on my phone alarm. 11:45 p.m. I had no idea how I'd managed to fall asleep, but somehow I'd drifted off and had been able to get at least a couple hours of rest.

I left my lamp off, in case Livvie decided to patrol the hallway, and turned on the bathroom light. I shut the door so that just enough light peeked through and slipped out of my oversize Hello Kitty sleep shirt and matching pink pants. I pulled out the clothes I'd so carefully borrowed from Paige's closet—a black cowl-neck sweater and dark-wash boot cut jeans—and paired them with my dark brown paddock boots.

In the bathroom, I ran my fingers through the tangled

waves in my air-dried hair. Last, I needed Lip Smackers. A quick coat of Wild Raspberry and I was ready.

I stuffed my keys and phone into my pocket. The door creaked as I eased it open and I held my breath. The hallway was dark, except for the low-lit wall fixtures that cast amber-colored light up the walls.

No sign of Livvie.

I pulled the door shut behind me and tiptoed down the hallway. I barely allowed myself to breathe until I'd stepped outside. The freezing air made me shiver. I stuck my hands in my pockets and started across campus. I avoided the streetlamps and darted across the courtyard. Being alone in the dark made me jumpy.

I wasn't used to the stable yard being so dark. It felt miles away from Winchester and the stable seemed to loom in front of me—magnified by shadows. I flicked open my phone and used it as a flashlight.

"Give me that!" a voice hissed. Someone snatched my phone from my hand.

"Hey!" I turned to see Georgia's face illuminated by the moonlight.

"Are you trying to get us caught?" she asked.

"I was trying not to trip!"

"Fine," she said, handing me back my phone. "Keep

that off. As soon as everyone else gets here, we'll get started. Violet and Brianna are waiting."

We stood in the frigid air. Soon, Callie, Julia, Alison, and Heather had joined us.

Callie gave me a half smile, but it vanished when she saw Heather walk over to stand by me.

"Ready?" Georgia asked.

We nodded.

"Then follow me."

We crossed the stable's driveway and walked around to the side that faced away from the campus. As we rounded the corner, I saw the glow of a warm light. Three battery-powered lanterns were placed along the ground. Beyond the lanterns, five horses were saddled and waiting. Black Jack. Aristocrat. Trix. Sunstruck. And Charm.

My. Horse. These girls had taken *my* horse from his stall and had saddled and bridled him. Beside me, Heather scoffed out loud.

"*Excuse* me," Heather said. Her loud voice seemed to shake the quiet of campus.

"Shhh!" said Brianna. She concentrated on holding Trix, Jack, and Sunstruck. Violet held Charm and Aristocrat.

Our horses were *not* happy. Their heads were up and

nostrils flared. Sunstruck danced in place and Brianna murmured something to him. None of the horses liked being in this strange place in the middle of the night. Neither did Callie, Heather, Alison, or Julia—I had a feeling.

"You took *my* Thoroughbred out of his stall without my permission," Heather said. "What gave you the right to do that?"

Empowered by Heather's attitude toward the older girls, I stood beside her and crossed my arms.

"You shouldn't have taken Charm out, either," I said. My voice was a little quieter than Heather's. "You didn't know how he'd react to strangers."

Violet handed Heather and me our horses' reins. "Relax. We know what we're doing. Your horses were lucky to be handled by us."

"Oh, really? Well—" Heather started.

"Hello. I think *I'm* talking now," Violet interrupted. Her gunmetal gray eyeliner made her eyes look colder somehow, steely.

Heather snapped her mouth shut, either in shock or fury, I wasn't sure which. I stood between her and Callie. "Mount your horses and we'll get started," Violet said.

Callie's eyes shifted to me for a second. Julia and

Alison looked at each other. Heather shook her head ever so slightly.

Callie was the first to move. She looked straight ahead, took a step back, and gathered Jack's reins in her hand. Then, she mounted. Julia and Alison followed her lead.

I looked up at Callie in disbelief. She'd gone way too far. I tried to ignore the wave of nausea in my stomach as I watched the three girls.

Heather looked at me, and I saw that look in her eyes—she wasn't going to back down. She wasn't going to let these girls bully her.

"No," Heather said. "I'm not getting on Aristocrat out here in the dark. It's dangerous for our horses."

Violet smiled, stepping forward until she was almost nose-to-nose with Heather.

"Really?" she asked, her tone sweet. "I think you will. Because if you don't, I don't know, I'll have to anonymously text your charming father and send him the loveliest photo of you. It'll show him how you're spending your time these days. I'm sure he'd love to know what's distracting you from riding."

"Whatever. Like you even have his number," Heather said.

Violet opened her phone, scrolled to a number, and

shoved her phone in Heather's face. "School directory," she smiled.

Heather faltered. "Fine. But what picture could you possibly send him? My focus on riding is just as strong as ever."

Violet grinned and pressed a button on her phone before holding it up to Heather. "But I wonder, *Heather*, if your dad will believe you when he sees this picture of you and your boyfriend, Ben."

Heather tilted her head up, sneering. "My dad doesn't care if I have a boyfriend."

But we both knew he would. Even if Heather did break up with Ben, the way she claimed she would, Mr. Fox would still freak that she'd spent any time with a boy when he thought she should have been riding.

"All right," Violet said. "Let's see now." She started to punch in a number and I could almost feel Heather's heartbeat from a couple of feet away.

"Okay, okay!" Heather said. "I'll get on."

"Super!" Violet said. She clicked the phone shut and watched us. I didn't even want to know what dirt Violet had on me.

I stuck my foot in the stirrup and mounted. Charm shifted underneath me and tensed.

"Easy, easy," I soothed. "It's okay." But I didn't believe

my own words. I had to find a way to stall until I could find a way out of this.

Heather slid into Aristocrat's saddle and the five of us looked down on the Belles from our horses.

"That wasn't so bad, was it?" Violet asked. She picked up a lantern and held it in her hand. The light threw shadows on her face and Sunstruck snorted. Alison's Arabian was the spookiest of the group. I crossed my fingers that she'd be able to control him.

Julia's face paled as Trix started to strike the ground with her hoof. "Um, she's getting scared," Julia said. "Do I need to stay on?"

"Yes," Georgia said. "She's fine."

"Let's get started on your task, shall we?" Violet asked. "It'll only take each of you a couple of minutes. I don't think I need to remind you that if you don't do as we ask, your position on the seventh-grade advanced team will be in jeopardy."

Sunstruck shifted sideways and bumped into Jack.

"Sorry," Alison told Callie. But Jack, the steadiest of the horses, didn't even blink.

"Want me to help hold him?" Callie asked.

Alison shook her head. She couldn't even look up. She was too busy circling Sunstruck. The palomino gleamed under the moonlight. He snorted and half-reared.

"Need help?" Heather called. She edged Aristocrat in front of Charm so she could see Sunstruck.

"No," Alison said. "He's fiiiinne!" Alison's last word turned into a shriek as Sunstruck trembled and threw himself backward. He rocked back on his haunches and his forelegs lifted off the ground.

"Lean forward!" Callie screamed.

Alison grabbed for Sunstruck's mane and tried to keep herself from sliding backward as he reared. My breath stopped as his hooves sliced through the air and he seemed to reach the sky.

Alison threw her weight against his neck and tried to force him to the ground. Heather urged Aristocrat forward and darted around Sunstruck's striking forelegs. She reached out and grabbed a rein. She yanked on it and Sunstruck finally thudded to the ground.

"Oh, my God, thank you," Alison said to Heather. Her face was ghostly white.

"I'm not letting go yet," Heather soothed. Sunstruck nosed Aristocrat and Heather's sometimes snobby gelding seemed to tell Sunstruck to calm down.

"You're so lucky we didn't see that happen *before* we asked you here," Violet groused.

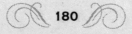

I couldn't believe her indifference. She couldn't at least acknowledge that Sunstruck could have flipped on Alison and crushed her? He could have thrown her and galloped off in the dark!

"Let's just get this done," Violet said.

I gripped Charm's reins, wishing I'd never come.

"You're each going to ride your horse from here to the admissions building," Violet said.

We looked at her like she was crazy.

"You'll brush the main door with your fingers and canter back," Violet added.

"We'll get caught!" Julia said, her voice small. "There are cameras and streetlamps everywhere."

"If you ride on the far left side of the sidewalk," Georgia said. "You won't get caught in the light, and the cameras won't pick up the image."

That was it—I couldn't keep my mouth shut any longer. Violet could do whatever she wanted to me, but Charm was off-limits.

"I won't risk Charm on a dare," I said. "He could wrench an ankle or slip in the dark."

Violet lifted up the lantern and smiled at me. "Sasha, if you're worried, you can leave. No one's keeping you here. But I know things about you, too." She walked by and whispered something in my ear, so quiet no one but I could hear it. Something that I couldn't quite decipher at first. But then, slowly, it dawned on me. At first, I'd thought she'd asked me if I'd read any good mail lately. But that wasn't it. What she'd said was, *Written any good e-mails lately?*

Violet's eyes roamed over Julia, Callie, and Alison. "I have secrets to spill about *all* of you."

But she couldn't. How could she know about my e-mail to Jacob? *Think!* I screamed to myself. *Come up with something—anything!*

"Let me ask each of you again," Violet said. "Are you going to do the dare—yes or no?"

All three girls stood in front of us. "Callie, yes or no?" Violet asked.

Callie hesitated and I felt her eyes on me for a second. She was actually considering risking Black Jack for this. Callie was smart, but she was also supercompetitive.

"Yes," Callie mumbled.

I shook my head in disbelief. I didn't even know my own friend anymore.

"Julia?" Brianna asked.

Julia nodded. "Yes."

"Alison?" Georgia asked.

"Yes," Alison said.

I squeezed my eyes shut for a second. I didn't know if Alison could control an already excited Sunstruck.

Charm strained his neck toward the stable and I had to hold him back. He wanted to go back in his snug stall and get out of the cold.

"Heather?" Violet's voice was calm.

"*No,*" Heather said. She didn't even think about it. She was going to let Violet text her dad to save Aristocrat from potential danger.

Violet turned to me. "Sasha?"

"No," I said. Violet could tell people whatever she wanted about me—I didn't care. Nothing was worth risking Charm.

Heather threw me a relieved smile.

"Fine," Violet said. "We have three smart girls and two who chose to be miserable for the next few months. Too bad. I'd hoped we could all be friends." She turned and pointed to Alison. "You're up first. Your horse needs to blow off some energy."

Alison didn't move.

"C'mon!" Brianna said. "We don't want to be out here all night."

Alison gathered Sunstruck's reins and he pranced

under her. The reins seesawed against his neck as he jerked his head up and down. If she was going to do this, I had to say something. Alison couldn't ride Sunstruck around in the dark. If he spooked, he could run off campus and head for the road. Alison would never forgive herself if something happened to him.

"Wait—" I started.

But Alison steadied herself in the saddle.

Suddenly, a giant beam of light flooded over us. "Everyone freeze. Now."

Someone walked toward us and one of the Belles' lanterns lit his face.

Oh, my God.

Mr. Conner.

We were so dead. Half of me wanted to hug him for stopping us before something serious happened. But the other half was terrified because I knew we were in *huge* trouble.

Mr. Conner lowered his flashlight from our faces and stepped up to us.

"Dismount right now," he said.

My legs shook as I got out of the saddle. My knees almost buckled under my weight.

No one said a word. We had no excuses for this and we knew it.

"You three," he pointed to Brianna, Violet, and Georgia. "Go straight to my office. The rest of you get those horses untacked and then join us."

He folded his arms and waited. The Belles started toward the stable. One by one, we led our horses past Mr. Conner.

I felt sick with embarrassment and anger. I should have said no the second the Belles had approached me. If I'd done the right thing, Charm and I wouldn't be in this mess.

The sound of the horses' hooves striking the ground was almost deafening in the still stable. I wondered if I'd be allowed back inside after tonight.

25

BANNED

THE WAIT OUTSIDE MR. CONNER'S OFFICE TOOK longer than forever. He hadn't emerged since he'd joined the Belles inside. Heather was slumped against the wall a few feet away from me. Julia and Alison stood by Callie, who rubbed her tear-streaked face with her hands.

I had a feeling none of us had ever been in this much trouble before.

Mr. Conner's office door opened. "Come in," he called.

For a second, none of us moved. But it was Heather who walked in first and the rest of us followed her. I could feel my heart beating in my throat. Mr. Conner's office, a place I'd been a million times by now, looked totally distorted and different through my complete and utter anxiousness. The Belles, who stood in front of Mr.

Conner's desk, shifted to the side so we could stand beside them.

Mr. Conner didn't offer anyone a chair—I knew he wanted us to stand in front of him.

"One of you needs to start talking," Mr. Conner said, directing his comment to the seventh graders.

Violet's eyes flashed as she looked at us. Callie glared right back and then looked at Mr. Conner.

"Violet, Brianna, and Georgia asked us to meet them here," Callie said. "They said if we didn't ride our horses in the dark, they'd hurt our positions on the advanced team."

"We *never*—" Violet started. Mr. Conner held up a hand.

"You could have said no," Mr. Conner said. "You should have come to me if you believed your future on the team was threatened."

"We should have," Heather said. "But we didn't. We didn't know what they wanted at first and then things just happened really fast."

"Mr. Conner," Violet protested. "We never made them do anything. They showed up on their own."

"With their horses?" Mr. Conner asked.

Violet's head jerked back a fraction. "No," she whispered.

Brianna and Georgia's shoulders sagged.

"The fact that you five even chose to mount your horses saddens me," Mr. Conner said. "But it concerns me much more that my *eighth*-grade advanced team dreamed up a dare that involved such a dangerous stunt—with horses. What would have happened had I not shown up?" Mr. Conner asked.

Our eyes shifted to the ground.

"Let me ask again," Mr. Conner's voice was cold. "What was the dare?"

The Belles shifted in their seats. Violet's chest rose and fell as she took in a shuddering breath.

"We dared them to canter their horses from the stable yard to the admissions building," Violet said. "They had to touch the door and ride back."

I couldn't believe she confessed. And, by the looks on their faces, neither could Georgia or Brianna.

"Riding in the dark," Mr. Conner murmured.

"Mr. Conner, we're so sorry," Violet said. Her eyes were pink and there was nothing fake about her reaction. "Brianna, Georgia, and I love horses. It was a stupid dare, and we're really sorry. We never intended for anyone— horse or rider—to get hurt. And, if it matters, not everyone agreed to do it."

Brianna and Georgia nodded while Heather and I exchanged a surprised glance.

"I'd like everyone to step outside my office for a moment," Mr. Conner said. "Sasha, please stay."

Me? Why me?

Callie's eyes widened and she looked at me. I could tell that she was afraid I'd tell Mr. Conner that she'd said yes to the dare. I looked away.

The other girls shuffled out of the office, and shut the door behind them. Mr. Conner sat down at his chair and gestured for me to sit on the chair across from his desk. For the first time tonight, I noticed the sadness and weariness in his eyes. My heart lurched. Mr. Conner was tough, but he was a good coach with a kind heart. I felt disgusted with myself for disappointing him after all he'd taught me.

"Sasha, I need to know if anyone would have actually ridden their horse," Mr. Conner said. He interlaced his fingers and placed his hands on his desk.

I thought for a minute. Even though Julia and Alison would have ratted me out, I wasn't sure I could do it to them. Plus, if I gave them up, I'd have to tell him about Callie, too. But maybe, I thought, I couldn't protect her from her own decision.

"I'm sorry for putting you in this difficult position," Mr. Conner said. "But these are riders on my advanced team. Rest assured, I won't reveal to anyone what you tell me. I need to know—did anyone agree to do the dare?"

I looked at the tops of my paddock boots. He wasn't going to let me leave unless I told him. And what if he thought that *I'd* considered the dare? He'd never trust me again if I didn't tell him the truth.

"Sasha, I'm only asking because I need to know for the future safety of the horses," Mr. Conner said.

I took a breath and closed my eyes for a second. Callie, Julia, and Alison had made their own decisions. I couldn't jeopardize Mr. Conner's trust in me.

"Yes," I said. I couldn't look him in the eye. "Callie, Alison, and Julia said yes. Heather and I said no."

I felt nauseated as I said Callie's name. Even after everything, I didn't want to hurt her.

"Thank you," Mr. Conner said. The hard look on his face started to fade. "Please join everyone else outside. I'll call you all back in a few minutes."

I left his office and closed the door behind me. Violet, Brianna, and Georgia were huddled together. Their smirks had long since vanished—I had a feeling they regretted this night as much as I did.

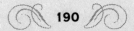

Callie left her spot by Julia and Alison. She stood inches away from me and looked like she was about to say something when she started to cry instead. Without thinking, I grabbed her into a tight hug. She hugged me back.

"I'm so embarrassed," Callie whispered. "I can't believe I was actually going to risk Jack for something so dumb! What kind of person am I?"

"You're not a bad person," I said, pulling back so I could see Callie's face. "We all got caught up in it."

"But *you* said no. Even Heather said no." Callie sniffed. "I love Jack so much. I just feel so guilty."

I took Callie's hand and squeezed it. "I know you love him. You'd never intentionally hurt him."

"Did Mr. Conner ask you who agreed to ride?" Callie asked.

I nodded.

"You told him."

"Yes," I said softly.

Callie let out a shaky sigh. "I'm not mad at you for telling him. I was going to confess anyway."

"But I'm still sorry I told him," I said. Out of the corner of my eye, I watched Heather walk over to Julia and Alison. She whispered something to them. Callie's tears finally slowed. "I missed you so much," she said. "I can't believe you're being so nice to me right now."

"I just wish the whole Jacob and Eric thing had never happened," I told her. "I should have tried harder to convince you that I was never with Eric. I kept saying no, but I don't blame you for not believing me. Eric and I have become really close friends, so we hung out together a lot."

A look flickered in Callie's eyes. "You really never were with Eric, were you?"

"Never," I said. "Not a second. I knew how much you liked him—I'd never hurt you that way."

"Oh, Sasha, I—" Callie started, but she stopped short. The Belles had walked over to us.

Violet clenched her hands together and looked at Brianna and Georgia before turning to us.

"Look . . . we're sorry," Violet said.

Julia and Alison, standing on either side of Heather, stepped closer to hear.

"I meant what I said to Mr. Conner," she said. "All three of us love horses and we value our spots on the team. We never should have put you or your horses at risk."

"Sorry," Brianna and Georgia echoed.

"What about the other stuff you said," Heather

challenged. "About sending my dad the picture and . . ." She glanced my way. Heather knew that Violet had tried to blackmail me, too. But she hadn't heard what Violet had against me.

But before Violet could respond, Mr. Conner's door opened. "Girls, please come in," he said.

My stomach lurched as I walked inside. I had no idea what he'd say. He might even send us home from the clinic.

"I needed a few minutes to think about the consequences of your actions," he said. "What you did was dangerous and reckless. Behavior of that kind is not tolerated by me or Canterwood Crest Academy. You put yourselves and your horses at risk. I hope you're all aware of how disappointing it is as an instructor to have eight of your most promising riders engaged in such actions."

We all lowered our heads.

"Therefore, none of you will ride in the demonstration on Saturday. You are all banned from riding for two weeks and this incident will be reported to Headmistress Drake. I'll be calling each of your parents in the morning. I've already called your dorm monitors—they'll be waiting for you at your dorms. Now, please go back to your rooms."

No demonstration. No chance to show off for scouts. No more lessons. Nothing.

Without a word, we left his office. We were all silent as we headed to our dorms. The Belles disappeared and I lagged behind everyone else.

A couple of hours ago, the campus had felt spooky in the dark. Now, it just looked cold and deserted.

Callie, Heather, Julia, and Alison reached the fork in the sidewalk where they were supposed to split off for Orchard Hall.

"You know what this means," Heather said. She stopped and looked at all of us. "Jasmine gets to ride in the demo and we don't."

"I completely forgot about that," I said. "She's going to be so happy."

"We can't just give up," Callie said.

Alison snorted. "Mr. Conner won't change his mind."

"But Callie is right," Julia said. "There must be something we can do to convince Mr. Conner to let us ride in the demo. It's too important not to try."

"Let's meet tomorrow morning at nine in Orchard's common room," Heather said. "Everybody come with an idea. We can't give up."

We said good-bye to each other and I walked back to Winchester.

Today had been awful—but oddly, some good had

come of it. Callie and I were talking again and Heather was fighting to reassemble the Trio. Soon, we'd *all* have to work together to get back in the demo. I just hoped my parents would see the good, too. . . .

26

CHEERS
TO THE PLAN

DAYS TILL THE DEMO, 3
HOURS SINCE THE BIG DISASTER: 7

RIIIING! I REACHED FOR THE DORM PHONE
on my bedside table.

"Hello?" I mumbled.

"Sasha, your father and I just got a call from Mr.
Conner," Mom said.

I sat up and rubbed my eyes. My alarm clock said
7:57 a.m.

"Mom, I'm so sorry," I said. "I made a huge mistake. I
know I never should have sneaked out."

"You were on *horseback* at midnight, Sasha. Do you realize how dangerous that was?"

"I know! The whole thing was so dumb and I wish I'd never even gone."

"Sasha, you knew better," Mom said. "Why did you listen to those girls?"

I sighed. "I don't know . . . I guess sometimes, it just feels like I'll never catch up to Callie or Heather. They're so good and no matter what, I don't have their training. I just wanted to fit in with the other girls."

"Sweetie," Mom said. "You're all on the advanced team. You're *just* as good as they are and you work hard. Don't let anyone make you feel insecure."

"Thanks, Mom."

"Don't think you're off the hook, young lady. It'll take time for your dad, Mr. Conner, and me to trust you again," Mom said. "You need to work hard to prove to Mr. Conner that he did the right thing by putting you on the advanced team. I am extremely disappointed. If you were home, I would ground you."

My stomach lurched. "I know. I'm sorry."

After we hung up, I headed for the shower. I needed to grab breakfast and start thinking about ways to prove myself to Mr. Conner.

*

At nine, Callie, Heather, Julia, Alison, and I gathered around the round table in Orchard's empty common room. A fire crackled in the fireplace and the room's cranberry colored walls felt warm and inviting.

Julia and Alison took seats on either side of Heather. I wondered if they'd made up?

Heather caught me staring.

"Sasha," she said. "Quit giving me the Bambi eyes. We made up. Deal with it."

Heather gave me the tiniest wink. For a second, I thought I'd imagined it. But then I realized—she'd confessed to Julia about why she'd stolen Ben. She'd actually taken my advice . . . and it had worked!

"Okay, let's focus," Alison said. "Mr. Conner *has* to lift the riding ban for Saturday." She straightened the neckline of her gold-flecked, off-the-shoulder white sweater. "If we can convince him to do that, we can promise him that we'll go right back to not riding for two weeks."

"But if we want him to agree to that, we have to prove ourselves all over again," I said. "How can we show him that we're sorry?"

Callie sipped her hot cocoa and put the cup back on the table. I sat back and tried to think of something.

"Chores!" Callie said, suddenly. "We should ask Mike

and Doug to give us work in the stable. If we muck, fill water buckets, feed the horses . . ."

"Mr. Conner will see how hard we're working," Julia finished. "It's perfect! He loves hard work."

Heather nodded and wrote *chores* on a piece of paper.

"Are we changing and then going to the stable?" Alison asked. "I'm not going near a horse in my new Sevens."

"Good idea," Heather said. "Let's meet at the stable in twenty minutes and get started. We don't have much time."

"We should be careful not to tell Jasmine what we're doing," I said. "If she finds out, she'll try to sabotage us."

"Let her think the chores are part of our punishment," Julia said.

"Here's to the plan," Callie said, raising her cocoa. The rest of us picked up our paper cups. "Let's hope the blisters, sore backs, and pounds of sawdust in our boots pay off."

We touched our cups together and I crossed my fingers for our plan to work.

"You're asking *me* to give *you* chores?" Mike asked, looking at the Trio, Callie, and me suspiciously.

"We need to prove to Mr. Conner that we're sorry," Alison explained. "We thought we'd start with chores."

"Not a bad idea," Mike said. "There's a lot to be done around here."

"Tell us," Julia said.

Mike grinned. He was enjoying this way too much! "Okay, Sasha and Callie, you can start mucking at the first stall on the left aisle. Julia and Alison, the water buckets from stalls seven through eighteen need to be sanitized. Heather, we need grain mixed."

"Thanks, Mike," I said. "We're ready to work."

"I've never seen anyone so excited about chores before," he said, shaking his head as he walked away.

"Let's do this," Heather said.

We split up and headed off to our assigned stations. Callie and I grabbed a muck cart and pitchforks and got to work.

"We're gonna be here a while," I said.

"Forever," she added.

We shoveled and scooped for more than two hours. We fell into a rhythm and concentrated so hard, there was little conversation. I couldn't help noticing that Callie still hadn't said a word about her boyfriend, but I didn't bring it up. If we were really going to be friends again, she'd tell me eventually . . . I hoped.

"The stalls look great, girls," Mike said. He poked

his head over the door. "Take a break and get a drink."

Callie and I propped the pitchforks up against the stall wall and walked out of the stall. Callie eyed a tack trunk outside of the stall and plopped onto it.

"Can't . . . make it," she moaned.

"I'll get your soda," I said.

"I knew you were my BFF for a reason."

I grinned, feeling better than I had in weeks. Even the Jacob e-mail wasn't bothering me right now. "Be right back."

Inside the tack room, I grabbed two sodas out of the minifridge. The tack room door opened and Eric stepped inside.

"Hey," he said. "Going for a ride?"

I shook my head. Eric still didn't know about the Belles. I'd been too scared to tell him. Disappointed parents and Mr. Conner were bad enough—I didn't know if I could handle it from Eric, too. "I can't ride for two weeks."

He looked at me like I was kidding. "Why?"

I put down the sodas and looked at him. "Mr. Conner caught me at midnight on horseback. These older girls bullied my friends and me into getting on our horses. I wasn't going to ride, but it was bad enough that I got on Charm."

"Wow," Eric said, his eyes wide. "And you didn't tell me about any of it? Why?"

"I don't know. I should have. After it happened, I was afraid to tell you because I didn't want you to think I was reckless with Charm."

Eric stepped closer to me. "Sasha, I know you love Charm. You'd never hurt him. But what about *you*? You could have been hurt."

I blew out a breath. "Yeah, well, not being able to ride in the demo definitely hurts."

"I'm so sorry," Eric said. "Is there any way you could convince Mr. Conner to change his mind?"

"We're doing stable chores right now to prove to him that we're willing to work hard. I've got to get this soda to Callie—we've been mucking for a while."

Eric nodded. "Mr. Conner will like the chores idea."

"We hope so."

Eric followed me out of the tack room and down the aisle. For a second, I worried that Callie would freak when she saw us together. But, I reminded myself, we were past that.

"Hey," he said to Callie.

She smiled at him while opening her soda.

"I'm done for the day," Eric said. "Can I help you guys?"

"You don't have to," I said. "It's our fault, not yours."

He shook his head. "It's that or cleaning my dorm. Mucking might be easier."

We laughed.

"You sure?" Callie asked. "We have a looong way to go."

"I'm in," Eric said.

Callie and I finished our sodas and the three of us headed to stall number eight. With three pitchforks, the work went fast. We talked and joked as we worked and there wasn't a hint of awkwardness among the three of us.

"I'm getting too good at this," Eric said when we moved into our third stall.

"Mike better watch out or you'll steal his job," Callie teased.

The three of us smiled and kept mucking. Hours later, we finally finished.

"I can't believe you stayed so long," I said to Eric. "Thank you."

"Yeah, thanks," Callie added. "We wouldn't have finished half as fast without you."

"No problem," Eric said. "Good luck with Mr. Conner. See you later."

As Eric walked away, I found myself trying hard not to stare after him. He was an amazing friend. I could always count on him. And, I thought, Callie was crazy to turn him down.

27

MESSY—
THE NEW HOT

CALLIE AND I STRUGGLED TO KEEP FROM grinning when we met up with the Trio at the end of the aisle. Heather, Julia, and Alison looked exhausted. Bits of sticky grain clung to the front of Heather's coat. Julia and Alison's pants had wet patches from lugging water buckets.

"Oh, don't give us that look!" Heather snipped. "You guys certainly don't look any better."

"True," I said. "We're *all* allowed to look messy and gross—we *have* been here for hours."

"I've got to go shower and get something to eat or I'll die," Alison said dramatically.

"Me too," Julia said. Her short blond hair stuck up in funny tufts and she had dirt smudges on her cheek.

"Want to meet up and get pizza in Orchard or Winchester after our showers?" Callie suggested. "I still think we need to come up with something more than chores."

The Trio exchanged a look.

"Sure," Heather said finally. "Winchester in an hour?"

I nodded. "Sounds good."

The Trio and Callie started to walk toward Orchard.

"Hey, Callie?" I called after her.

She stopped and turned toward me. "Yeah?"

"Paige is in New York and my room is kinda lonely. Want to sleep over?"

Her smile turned into a giant grin. "Sure! I'll bring my stuff when I come over tonight. It'll be good to . . . you know, talk."

I smiled up at the sky and felt my tiredness start to ebb away as I walked. My best friend was back!

28

DEAR MR. CONNER

THE TRIO, CALLIE, AND I WERE GATHERED in Winchester. Callie had arrived first and we'd left her overnight bag in my room. We'd asked Livvie if we could order a pizza and she said she'd bring it to us when the delivery person got here. Livvie would definitely be roaming the halls tonight—she had ever since Mr. Conner had informed her about my sneaking out.

Callie and I claimed the smaller sofa and Heather took the recliner by the fire. Julia and Alison sprawled out on the bigger couch.

"I'm so tired," I said, stifling a yawn.

"Me too," Callie said. "I could never do that job every single day."

"We're going to *have* to keep doing it unless we come up

with another way to impress Mr. Conner," Alison said.

"Hi, girls," Livvie said as she walked into the room. Steam filtered out through the pizza box holes and I inhaled the scent of cheesy goodness. She set the box on the counter and we stared at it with hungry eyes.

"Thanks, Livvie," we chorused.

"You're welcome," Livvie said before going back to her room.

I jumped off the couch and pulled out a stack of plates. Callie yanked open the pizza box. Everyone filled their plates and for a few minutes no one spoke as we shoved pizza into our mouths.

"I was thinking," I said, between bites. "Maybe our words aren't enough."

"What do you mean?" Alison asked, wiping sauce off her chin with a paper towel.

"Maybe we write him a letter," I said.

Callie put down her pizza and nodded. "That's not a bad idea! We could write it together and all sign it."

"Silver," Heather said. "You're not as dumb as I tell everyone you are."

I made a face and took another bite of pizza.

"That's definitely something Mr. Conner would respect," Julia agreed.

I ran and grabbed a piece of stationery and pen from my room and brought it back to the common room.

"Horse stationery?" Heather laughed, staring at the paper. "Geek much?"

But, as I organized the table so that we could write the letter, I caught her glancing at the back of the box and making a mental note of the company's logo. I had a feeling I'd be seeing the same stationery in her bag soon enough. . . .

"You write the letter," Heather told Alison. "Your handwriting is the best."

Alison took the pen and paper.

"Dear Mr. Conner," I said. Alison started scribbling as we all threw suggestions at her.

"Tell him we're sorry," Callie said.

"And we'll never do it again," Julia added.

"Make sure you remind him that we're serious riders," Heather said.

"Guys! I can't write that fast!" Alison protested. "Slow down."

We waited while she wrote down our ideas.

"There," Alison said a few minutes later. "How's that?"

We gathered around the paper. I leaned over Callie's shoulder and read it.

208

Dear Mr. Conner,
We know we can't apologize enough for what we
did. We've all worked too hard to throw it away
for something so stupid as a dare. Our horses
are one of the most important things in our lives
and we didn't act like it on Wednesday night.
We're sorry and embarrassed about what we did.
Through our future actions, we hope you'll learn
to trust us again. We promise to keep proving to
you that we're serious about the team and our
futures as riders.
Sincerely,
Alison, Heather, Callie, Sasha, and Julia

"Perfect," I said. "You guys think it's okay?"

Heather nodded. "Let's sign it and I'll drop it off at his office."

We took turns signing the paper.

"Even if he doesn't change his mind," Callie said. "I'm glad we wrote the letter. It made me feel a lot better."

"Me too," I agreed. "Hey, you guys want dessert?" I asked.

"Got any chocolate?" Callie asked.

"Brownies, M&Ms, cake, or chocolate-covered pretzels?" I rattled off.

"All of the above!" Alison said.

"I'll make up a tray of chocolate," I said, feeling very Paige-like.

I piled a serving tray with enough chocolate for a serious sugar high and set the tray down on the table.

"Thank you!" Callie said, grabbing a handful of pretzels.

Everyone, even Heather, ate as if we hadn't just devoured a whole pizza. Once we'd finished stuffing ourselves again, Heather pulled Julia and Alison up off the couch.

"We'll see you at the stable at seven to start working," Heather said. She paused. "That sounded *so* wrong."

Once they left, Callie and I flicked off the lights in the common room and headed to my room. We changed into our pj's—mine: a white long-sleeve shirt and pink and gray striped pants; Callie's: an oversize teal T-shirt, black leggings, and fuzzy lavender-colored socks. Callie climbed onto Paige's bed. She put her phone on the table between our beds and stared at it for a few seconds. Then, she grabbed it and put it beside her.

"It's not like you can't hear it ringing on the table," I joked.

"Oh, you're probably right," Callie said. She placed the phone facedown on the table. "You sure Paige doesn't mind that I'm sleeping in her bed?"

"No way," I said. "She's just glad you're sleeping over."

Callie got quiet. She grabbed Paige's pillow and hugged it to her chest. "Yeah. I'm happy, too."

I couldn't help thinking that Callie wasn't exactly acting like herself—she was being a little weird. Or maybe . . .

"Do you miss Julia and Alison?" I asked.

Callie snorted. "Are you kidding me? I'm glad things are getting back to normal."

"Me too," I said, flicking on the TV.

"What's tonight's movie?" Callie asked.

"I Tivoed the new Cameron Bowen flick!"

"Oooh! Yes! I've been dying to see that."

Cam always put Callie in a good mood. I turned on the TV and Callie and I scooted to the ends of our beds, giggling.

"When school starts again, we have to do this at least, I don't know, every single weekend," I said.

"For sure," Callie agreed. We settled into our beds and got ready for ninety minutes of eye-candy Cameron.

When the credits started to roll, Callie and I let out sighs.

"I could watch him all day," I said.

"Yeah," she said.

"Yeah," I repeated.

But I couldn't stand it anymore!

"So, does your boyfriend look anything like Cam?" I asked.

Callie's head whipped around and she stared at me, wide-eyed. "What? Who told you I had a boyfriend?"

"I can just tell," I said, improvising. I didn't want to tell her I'd been eavesdropping on Julia and Alison. "You're acting different—secret texting, makeup, new clothes . . ." I let my sentence trail off. "There has to be a guy."

"Yeah . . . there is a guy," Callie said slowly.

"Callie! You owe me details. *Lots* of details. Where'd you meet him? What does he look like? What's his *name*?"

Callie ignored me and climbed under the covers. "Sorry, but I got really tired all of the sudden. Let's go to sleep and talk about it later."

"Callie!" I squealed. "Tell me!"

"Seriously, I'm really tired," she said. "I think I made myself sick with all that junk food. I just need to sleep."

"Oh." I shrugged and got into my bed. "Okay. 'Night."

I flicked off the light. What had just happened? We'd been having so much fun and then she'd shut me out. I stared at the darkening ceiling.

"Sasha, I'm sorry." Callie's voice was barely a whisper. "It's just . . . I need to tell you . . ."

I waited for Callie to finish her sentence, but she didn't say anything.

"Cal?"

"Never mind. 'Night."

Our unfinished conversation kept me awake long after Callie fell asleep. There was no reason for her not to want to talk about her boyfriend. Unless . . . she didn't want to because she thought it would make me feel bad, since things with Jacob were so weird.

That was it! She didn't want me to feel bad about not having a boyfriend while she had one. I let out a happy sigh. *That* was a good friend.

29

A VERDICT

MR. CONNER'S CLINIC, DAY 12
DAYS LEFT UNTIL DEMO: 1
STALLS LEFT TO MUCK: 23
SENTENCES CALLIE STARTED AND NEVER FINISHED
IN THE LAST 48 HOURS: 10
TIMES I VOWED NOT TO THINK ABOUT JACOB AND FAILED:
INFINITY

AT SEVEN THE NEXT MORNING, CALLIE AND I
walked to the stable together. We'd chatted about random
stuff while we'd gotten dressed this morning and breakfast hadn't been any different.

"Ready for another day of labor?" I asked.

Callie flexed her arm. "Bring it!"

The Trio walked in a few seconds later and we found
Mike filling water buckets.

"Back again?" he asked, seeming surprised.

"Tell us what to do," Heather said. "We're ready."

Mike put Heather and Callie on mucking duty, Alison on feeding. Julia and I had to check the hay bales in the loft for mold.

"Did Mr. Conner say anything about our work yesterday?" Julia asked Mike.

"Sorry," Mike said. "He didn't mention it."

"Oh," Callie said. We exchanged frowns.

"Keep at it," Mike said. "You're doing the right thing." He turned on the hose and started refilling buckets.

"Let's go," Julia said. I followed her and we split off from everyone.

Julia and I climbed into the loft and stared at the hundreds of bales. We had to sniff, touch, and inspect each one. Hay was supposed to smell sweet and fresh. If it smelled musty or weird, it got tossed. Moldy hay could cause severe colic or even death. I felt proud that Mike had trusted us enough to give us a serious job.

"Want to start at opposite ends and work our way to the middle?" Julia asked.

I nodded. "Sounds good."

I bent down by the first bale and took a deep sniff. Sweet. I stuck my hand into the bale and it felt dry and cool—the way it should feel. On to the next bale. I

repeated my sniffing and feeling process until I'd made a small dent in the pile.

"Are you glad to have Heather back?" I asked Julia.

She gave me a withering stare. "Why do you care?"

"Just wondering. I'm glad we're all working it out for the team."

"*We're fine,*" Julia said. "But *you're* not."

"What is *that* supposed to mean? Callie and I are friends again."

Julia tested another bale before looking up at me. "You don't want Callie back. Trust me."

"Because she bad-mouthed me about stealing Eric? Yeah, that was wrong, but I'm over it. It's not worth it."

Julia shook her head. "Whatever you say."

I moved away from her and went back to work. Julia was obviously jealous that Callie and I were friends again. But what did *she* care? She and Heather had made up, too.

I sneezed and two seconds later, Julia did the same.

"Think it's time to take a break?" I called.

"Yes!" Julia said, sneezing again.

We walked down the aisle and found Callie and Heather spreading clean sawdust around a just-mucked stall.

"Break for sodas?" I asked them.

Callie nodded and stood her pitchfork up against the wall. "Yes!"

Alison walked over to us. "My arms are about to fall off from lugging buckets," she whined.

"I think I've got four pounds of hay dust up my nose," I added.

"Aw, look at this," said a snotty voice I knew too well.

We turned and saw Jasmine, one hand planted on her hip.

"What?" Alison snapped. "Is hard work something you've never seen before?"

Jasmine stared at Alison. "Unfortunately for you, I've been working hard for the clinic. But you all won't be at the demo, so you won't be able to see that for yourselves. How sad!"

It took everything I had to keep my mouth shut. "You're right," I said, trying as hard as I could to make it sound like none of this was any big deal. "We'll be doing stable chores all day Saturday."

"Sounds like fun," Jasmine said, wiggling her fingers at us as she walked away.

"I *so* hope we're riding tomorrow," Julia whispered as she stepped out of the stall. "We need to take her down!"

We giggled and walked down the aisle to get sodas. We

reached the end of the row when Doug called after us.

"Mr. Conner wants to see you all in his office," Doug said.

"What if he doesn't lift the ban?" Alison whispered. "Then what?"

"Then we won't be in the demo," Heather said. "That's it."

I fumbled in my pocket for a lip gloss—grabbed my Kiss This Gloss in Tickle—and rubbed it over my lips for extra confidence.

"Let's go," I said. We walked to Mr. Conner's closed office door and stood there for almost a full minute before Callie finally knocked on the door.

"Come in," Mr. Conner said.

Alison pushed the door open and we filed inside. My heart rate sped up. This was it. He'd either tell us our obvious attempts at impressing him weren't working or he'd lift our riding ban.

He looked up from the paper he was reading and put down his pen. I saw the first handwritten line, *Dear Mr. Conner*. Then I saw our names at the bottom. He was reading our letter!

"I noticed that you've been working around the stable," he said.

We nodded.

"Mike and Doug have been keeping me updated on all of the work you've done," Mr. Conner said. "Obviously an attempt to get permission to ride."

I squeezed my hands together, feeling more than a little deflated. After all of the work we'd put in, he hadn't been impressed at all.

"With that said, your work ethic impressed me. I've also read your letter. Your actions since Wednesday night have spoken of your true characters."

"We just wanted you to know how sorry we are," Callie said.

"I know you're sorry," Mr. Conner said. "There are noticeable differences between you five and the other students involved in this incident."

Mr. Conner held up the letter. "You're making an effort to *show* me you're sorry, instead of just saying it. You wrote a letter and you've been working hard for two days. Have you seen the other girls working in the stable?"

"No," Heather said.

I elbowed her. That had been a rhetorical question!

"You've all worked to prove you're sorry. I'm impressed by your dedication."

I tried not to smile. He was going to lift the ban! I knew it!

"I wish I could erase your two-week riding ban," he said. "But I'm afraid I can't."

My shoulders slumped. No! We were going to miss the demo. Our chance at riding for the scouts—gone. I bit my lower lip, struggling not to cry.

Mr. Conner looked at us. "I can, however, lift your ban for two days."

"Oh, my God!" Alison blurted out.

We grinned and Julia grabbed her hand.

"You may all ride in the demo, but after that, it's back to no riding for the rest of the two weeks. Deal?" Mr. Conner asked.

"YES!" We all shouted at the same time.

He laughed. "Good. Lessons are over now, but you may use the indoor arena for the rest of the afternoon if you want to practice."

"Thank you, thank you!" I said.

"Really, thank you!" Julia added.

Mr. Conner nodded. "You're welcome. I'll be sure to call your parents to tell them about your efforts. Now get practicing. And don't forget—you're representing Canterwood tomorrow. Make me proud."

We gave him giant smiles and tried to get out of his office so fast, we all almost got stuck in the doorjamb!

Once the door closed, we grabbed each other in a group hug. "We did it!" I cheered. "We're riding in the demo!"

"Let's tack up and get riding!" Callie said.

"Wait," Heather said. Her smile disappeared. "If you *ever* tell anyone I participated in a group hug, you will die. Got it?"

"What group hug?" I asked, sticking my tongue out at Heather.

We bolted for the tack room and grabbed our gear.

"Charm!" I said when I reached his stall. "Guess what?"

Charm nuzzled me as I clipped the lead line to his halter. "We're in the demo! We get to ride for the scouts!"

Charm rubbed his head on my arm and I hugged his neck. "We have to work hard, boy," I said. "Tomorrow's our big chance."

30

HEATHER— THE NEW MR. CONNER

I BUCKLED MY HELMET INTO PLACE AND LED Charm up to Jack.

"Charm's going to freak out when he realizes we're practicing together," I told Callie. "He's missed Jack a lot."

"Jack's going to be happy, too," she said.

We had just joined the Trio inside the arena when Jasmine rounded the corner.

"Can't stop breaking the rules, can you?" she asked.

"Why are you stalking us?" Heather snapped.

"Oh, please, you're hardly worth stalking," Jasmine said. "Trust me, I just have good timing. I'm sure Mr. Conner will *love* hearing about this."

I led Charm around her. "I'm sure he will! Be sure to

tell him we said thanks again for letting us ride in the demo."

"Bye," Callie said, mimicking the little wave Jasmine had given us earlier.

We laughed and led our horses into the arena for a warm-up. We walked, trotted and cantered a few times around the arena. Charm, a few strides behind Jack, lifted his hooves high and stretched his neck.

"Feels good, huh, boy?" I asked.

He snorted and I rubbed a hand over his neck.

"We've got to rock this tomorrow," Heather said, pulling Aristocrat to a walk.

"We will," Callie said. "Jasmine's so mad at us that she's going to push Phoenix and mess up. You know she will."

The arena door opened. I expected to see Jasmine stick her head in and spy on us. Instead, Eric walked through the door.

"Hey!" I said. I broke away from the group and rode up to him.

"You got the ban lifted?" he asked.

"Yes! We get to ride in the demo, then it's back to no riding. But I don't care. I mean, I do, but I'm excited that I get to ride for scouts."

Eric laughed. "Really? I couldn't tell at all that you're excited."

Charm stretched his neck out to Eric and got his blaze rubbed.

"Silver!" Heather called, giving me the evil eye. "We're on a limited practice time here. More riding, less talking!"

Yep, aside from no Jacob, things were *so* back to normal.

"Sorry," Eric said, loud enough so Heather could hear. "Mind if I watch?"

"Yeah, stay," I said. "I'd like that."

I rode Charm back to the rail and Eric grabbed a chair outside of the arena.

"Want to work on those jumps?" Heather asked. She nodded to four verticals Mr. Conner had set up on the right side of the arena.

"Sure," I said. Callie, Alison, and Julia agreed.

"I'm just going to do the course twice," Callie said. "I don't want Jack to be tired for tomorrow."

"Good idea," Alison said. "I'm not worried about Sunstruck, but *I'll* be tired tomorrow if I don't stop after that."

"Fine, wimps," Heather said. "Twice over the course and we'll stop."

"I'll go first," Julia said. She circled Trix and then pointed her at the course. Trix's short but powerful legs propelled her over the three-foot-high verticals and they finished quickly.

"Nice," Alison said. "Just watch that she doesn't weave between fences."

Julia nodded. "Good point. If you see her do it next time, tell me."

Alison gathered Sunstruck and let the gelding canter up to the first red and white vertical. His pale tail swished behind him and he leapt over the plastic rail with inches to spare. Alison knew how to keep him calm as they bounded over the jumps. They finished without tapping even one rail.

"Perfect," Callie cheered. "He's all business today, isn't he?"

Alison nodded. "Maybe the time off was good for him."

"Go ahead," Callie said to me. "I'll go last."

"Okay." I pushed my heels down and Charm moved out into a smooth canter. I counted down the strides— *four, three, two, one, and up!* On up, I lifted out of the saddle and moved my hands along Charm's neck. He rounded his back and rose into the air. We landed and in four strides, he leapt the second vertical.

I did a half-halt to slow him and he eased up.

"Good boy," I whispered. I rocked in the saddle and leaned forward as he jumped the third vertical. He took them with such ease. We cantered to the final jump and he seemed suspended in air until his front hooves hit the ground.

I turned Charm and Callie clapped.

I glanced over at Eric. He gave me a thumbs up and a big smile.

Callie rode Jack forward to the course. The Morab moved as if he jumped like this in his sleep. Callie completed the course without a wobble and rode back with a smile.

"*That* felt good," she said.

"It'll feel better after we do it AGAIN," Heather said.

"Yes, Mr. Conner," I teased.

Even Heather smiled at that. "Fine," she said. "Then I'll take it all the way."

She turned to Julia. "Go again. This time, more leg before Trix takes off. Don't jerk on her mouth when you land. Got it?" She mimicked Mr. Conner's deep voice.

"Yes, sir," Julia said.

I sat back in the saddle and waited for my turn. Out of the corner of my eye, I watched Eric. He almost jumped

up in his seat every time one of the horses launched into the air. I laughed to myself. It was like he was riding the course, too!

After we'd all finished, we dismounted and cooled the horses. The horses were ready to get back to their stalls and I had a feeling we all wanted to go back to our rooms. Eric, probably afraid of incurring Heather's wrath, waved goodbye and slipped out of the arena.

The Trio led their horses out of the arena first and Callie and I followed behind them. Callie's eyes were on the ground. She must have been stressing about tomorrow.

"We'll be ready for the demo," I said. "It'll be okay."

"Oh," she said. "I know. I mean, you're right. I mean . . . see you tomorrow."

"Oh," I said. "Okay."

It's just nerves, I reminded myself. *Just nerves.*

"I can't wait to see you tomorrow!" Paige said, via Webcam.

"I know! It's going to be awesome to have you at the demo!"

Paige grimaced. "I might have to cover my eyes, though, when you go over those giant jumps. I'm scared just watching you!"

"I'll be fine," I laughed. "Charm takes care of me."

"Go get some sleep," Paige said. "See you in the morning."

"See you then." I flicked off the camera and went to my closet. I needed an outfit that screamed *Future YENT Member.*

I looked through my show breeches and picked a fawn colored pair with suede knees. My tall show boots were shiny since I'd cleaned them after my last event. I grabbed a white show shirt and my favorite show coat—the black one with the gold stitching—and put everything together on my bed. I stepped back to look at it.

Perfect. Charm and I would be ready.

31
DON'T BLOW IT

IT WAS JUST BEFORE EIGHT ON SATURDAY morning and the demo started at nine. The groups were staggered, so I didn't technically go on until nine thirty.

A handful of cars and SUVs filled the parking lot. I wondered if any of them belonged to scouts. I hurried into the stable and almost got run over by a girl running out the door.

"Sorry!" she said. "Forgot my choker pin!"

I touched my neck to be sure my pin was there. I'd thrown on an oversize sweatshirt and sweatpants over my show clothes. As much as I loved Charm, I couldn't trust him not to sneeze on me.

I walked to the indoor arena where the riders were supposed to gather for a final pep talk from the instructors.

"Welcome," Mr. Conner said after everyone had gathered inside. "I want to thank you for attending our clinic. I hope you feel prepared for today's demonstration. You've all shown tremendous growth. I look forward to hearing of your successes in the equestrian circuit."

"Best of luck to all of you," Miss Cho said. "Thank you for your hard work."

Mr. Bright stepped forward. "I thank you all for your well-wishes for my daughter. Thankfully, she'll make a full recovery. I hope her accident serves as a reminder to us to be careful riders."

Ms. Thorne stared at us and smiled. "If I see any poor jump seats," she warned. "I'll stay an extra day just to make you jump without stirrups again."

We all laughed.

"Go get ready and good luck!" Mr. Conner said.

Everyone rushed to the door. I grabbed Charm's tack box before going to his stall.

"You okay?" I asked him. His ears flicked back and forth and his bottom lip trembled. "Don't get nervous.

Maybe I'll just groom you in your stall so we stay away from all of the craziness out there."

I went into his stall and clipped a lead line to his halter. I tied him to the iron bars on his stall and picked up the hoof pick.

"Ready for your predemo grooming?"

Charm nodded.

I blocked out the nervous chatter of other riders and focused on Charm. After I picked his hooves, I brushed him until every hair on his coat gleamed. I rubbed his face with a clean cloth and he closed his eyes. He stood still, almost sleeping, while I combed his mane and detangled his tail.

I took his tack box out of the stall and checked to see if crossties were free. A pair a few stalls down was empty.

"C'mon, boy," I said to Charm, leading him down the aisle. I clipped him into the ties.

"Hey," Callie said. She and Jack walked up to me.

I finished a final sweep of Charm's coat with a soft cloth while Callie put Jack on a tie ring.

"Do you feel ready?" I asked Callie.

"As much as I can be," she said. "You?"

"A little nervous, but yeah, I think we'll be fine."

My phone buzzed and I looked at the screen. *I'm here!*

"Oh, my God!" I said. "Paige is here!"

"Go say hi to her," Callie said. "I'll watch Charm."

"Be right back."

I hurried outside to look for Paige. The yard was full of students, horses, and adults. Ms. Thorne stood by the arena and talked to a man in a black suit. Maybe he was a scout. By the stone benches, I saw Paige crane her neck and look around.

"Paige!" I called.

She turned and saw me. "Sasha!"

"You look amazing," I said, giving her a hug. "Your coat is gorgeous."

Paige wore a plum-colored wrap coat, skinny jeans, and furry chocolate-brown boots.

"Thanks. It's from the *Teen Cuisine* wardrobe. I *might* have snagged you a few accessories."

"Omigod!" I hugged her again and she laughed.

"Take me to see Charm! I haven't seen him in a while," Paige said.

Paige and I linked arms and headed for the stable.

"Welcome back," Callie said, hugging Paige.

"It's good be back," Paige said, stretching out a hand to Charm. "Hi, beautiful."

Charm sniffed Paige's hand and she stepped up to rub

his neck. Paige looked over and saw Jack. "He looks gorgeous, too, Callie."

"Thanks," Callie said.

"Here, girls," Mike said, walking up to us. He carried my saddle, bridle, and saddle pad on his right arm and Callie's on his left.

"Thanks, Mike," I said.

"Yeah, you didn't have to do that," Callie said. We took our tack from Mike.

"You both deserve a little help after doing so many of *my* chores," Mike said. "Good luck."

He walked off and Paige looked at me. "Chores? What's he talking about?"

Callie and I looked at each other and then at Paige.

"It's kind of a long story," I said.

"Yeah, long and one that has to be told over hot chocolate," Callie said.

Paige squinted at us. "You guys did something. You *have* to tell me after the demo."

"Promise," I said. "We've got to tack up. Do you want to go find a seat in the indoor arena?"

"Sure," Paige said. "I know you guys don't need it, but good luck!"

Paige walked away and Callie and I got to work.

"We have to take her on a trail ride soon," Callie said. "I'm sure Mr. Conner would let her ride a stable horse."

"Yeah—that would be so much fun," I said. "She'd love it."

I smoothed the pad onto Charm's back and placed the saddle on top of it. I reached under his stomach for the girth and tightened it. Charm didn't move while I unclipped the crossties and slipped the reins over his head. Callie and I finished bridling the horses at the same time.

"Oops!" I said. "Forgot to paint his hooves."

"Here." Callie tossed me her hoof polish.

"Thanks." I bent down and smoothed on a clear layer of polish. "Now, we're ready."

I started to lead Charm away from the crossties.

"Um, Sasha?" Callie said.

"What?"

"Our clothes."

I looked down at my sweats.

Oops!

"Right." I handed her Charm's reins and she held him while I peeled off my sweatpants and took off my sweat-shirt. Callie handed me back Charm's reins and I took Jack's while she stripped off her dirty clothes, revealing a perfectly tailored navy jacket and beige breeches.

 234

"Now we're ready," she said.

We looked at each other and I gave Callie an encouraging smile.

"Let's do it," she said.

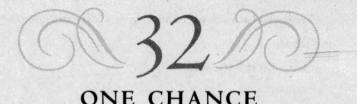

32

ONE CHANCE

HORSES AND RIDERS PACKED THE WAITING area near the indoor arena. Riders muttered strategies under their breaths, readjusted leg wraps, and brushed horsehair off show coats.

"Let's keep them away from that for as long possible," Callie said. "They'll get nervous."

I scanned the aisle for a quiet spot. "Over there," I said. A space had emptied near the back. We led our horses away from the crowd and I rubbed Charm's shoulder.

"Do you remember how this is going to work?" I asked Callie. "I think I zoned out when Miss Cho explained it to my group."

"Ms. Thorne told us that each group would do flatwork first and then we'd talk to the scouts. After everyone does flatwork, we'll all move out to the jump course."

"Wait, we have to *talk* to them?" I stopped Charm and looked at Callie.

"Yeah, I think so."

From our spot, we could just see through the large window into the indoor arena. I peered through the glass and watched Heather's group trot, canter, halt, and reverse directions. For a minute, my nerves eased as I watched Heather ride.

She and Aristocrat made the other riders look as if they hadn't even attended the clinic. I shifted my eyes to the stands and focused on a group of people who had to be scouts. Four men and two women. They held clipboards and looked back and forth from the riders to their notes. A few seats in front of the scouts, Paige leaned forward in her chair and watched the riders.

After a few minutes, Miss Cho signaled Heather's group to stop. The students lined up their horses in the arena's center. Heather scratched Aristocrat's neck and he let out a quiet snort.

The scouts stood in their seats and walked toward the horses and riders. As a group, they moved together and stopped in front of Heather, who was first in line. They

studied Aristocrat and turned their heads as they whispered. One man said something to Heather. She nodded and whatever she said back made him smile.

The judges did the same to each person in line. When they looked to Mr. Conner, he stepped into the arena.

"If you'll take your horses back to the waiting area, we'll progress through the other four groups and then your group will be first to jump," Mr. Conner said. "Thank you."

The riders dismounted and led their horses out of the arena. Heather headed for Callie and me.

"You next?" she asked Callie.

"Yeah," Callie said, turning to Jack and preparing to mount.

Heather stopped Aristocrat. "Good luck. Oh, and Sasha, Julia told me she thought she saw Jacob outside."

"What?!" I shook my head. "He's here? Really? Where?"

"Oh my God, calm down," Heather said. "Julia said he was by the outdoor arena." She led Aristocrat away from us.

OMG! He came to watch me ride. He was going to tell me he wanted to be more than friends.

I checked my watch. "If I hurry, I can go find him and get back in time for my class."

"No," Callie said, stepping around Jack. "You can't. You could be late and miss your ride for the scouts. Mr. Conner would *freak* if you left."

I looked around for him. "But he's watching the other group ride. He won't notice if I'm gone for two minutes."

Callie narrowed her eyes at me. "After we just convinced Mr. Conner to let us ride, you're going to run off? Don't."

"But . . ."

I took a breath. She was right. Jacob could wait. This was more important. "Okay," I said. "I'll stay. You're right."

"Good," Callie said. "I would have worried too much about you being late."

Callie mounted Jack and turned him toward the arena. She pointed her crop at me. "Do. Not. Leave."

"Promise," I said. "Good luck!"

Callie rode into the arena with Julia, Alison, and another girl in their group. They were down a member since Georgia couldn't ride.

The second Jack started moving, I knew Callie had no reason to be worried. Her hands and legs were quiet as she guided him through Miss Cho's instructions. The scouts

didn't show any emotion while they watched Callie ride, but I could tell by the way they looked at her that they were impressed.

I tried to stay focused, but my mind couldn't help wandering. Jacob was here! As soon as I got through my flatwork round, he'd be waiting when Charm and I jumped. Charm and I would fly over the jumps, and Jacob would be so impressed.

Finally, Callie's group finished and the scouts strode up to her, Julia, Alison, and the other rider. It was time to prep for my ride.

"Good luck," Eric said, walking up beside Charm. He scratched Charm's shoulder. "I'm going to go grab a seat."

"Thanks," I said. "Paige is in there already."

Eric slipped away. I closed my eyes and visualized a good ride.

"I can't believe Mr. Conner let you in here," Jasmine snapped.

I kept my eyes closed for a few more seconds before looking at her. She led Phoenix over by Charm and me.

"I don't have time for this," I said. "I'm trying to get ready."

Jasmine brushed the sleeves of her hunter green show

coat. "Well, unlike you, I'm all ready. I got an extra day of lessons that *you* didn't get and I always rode after class. I'm more than prepared."

"You rode after lessons?" I asked. "When?"

"Every day," she said. "You ran out of here as fast as you could, but I actually stayed to practice more."

I turned away from her and mounted Charm. That's why I'd never seen her around campus or at the cafeteria. *I should have been here*, I thought. But instead, I'd been trail riding, getting in trouble, and obsessing about Jacob. And my mind was still stuck on him. It drove me crazy that he was out there and I was stuck in here!

Cole and Aaron mounted their horses and we waited for our signal to go in. Mr. Conner dismissed Callie's group and she and Jack walked by us.

"Amazing!" I said. I leaned down to slap Callie's palm.

"Thanks." She smiled up and me and patted my boot. "I know you'll do great."

Mr. Conner stuck his head out into the aisle. "Group C, we're ready for you."

Jasmine urged Phoenix in front of me and I rode in after her. Cole and Aaron followed me. The group felt noticeably smaller without Violet.

I tried to keep my hands from shaking.

"Hello, everyone," Miss Cho said to us. "Please move your horses along the wall and start at a walk."

Here we go! Just get through this and then you can ride and see Jacob.

I slid Charm behind Cole, who followed Jasmine. No way I wanted to be near *her*. She'd pull some dumb trick to mess me up. I kept my eyes focused between Charm's ears and didn't look at the scouts in the arena.

"Trot," Miss Cho called.

The second I touched my heels to his sides, Charm moved into a smooth trot. I posted and we made a couple of laps around the arena.

I almost couldn't hide my smile. This was going to be *waaay* easier than I'd thought. Charm could do these exercises without me! I wondered what Jacob was doing. I hoped he'd come inside the stable.

"Cross over the center and then canter at the wall," Miss Cho called.

Uh-oh . . . did she say walk through the center and halt at the wall?

I slowed Charm to a walk and we started across the arena. Everyone else kept trotting. My stomach twisted. Did I mess up the instructions?

"Trot, Sasha!" Miss Cho called.

I wanted to hide. That's just what I needed—to be called out in front of the scouts. No one else had missed the instructions.

I nudged Charm with my heels, but he ambled along at a walk. I squeezed my legs tighter around Charm's sides. He took five more strides at a walk before he broke into a bumpy trot. Charm trotted for only a few seconds before the rest of my group started to canter.

I nudged Charm with my toe behind the girth. He ducked his head and shook his mane. Two strides later, he started to canter and both ears pointed forward. He wasn't listening to me at all. I closed my fingers on the reins and tried to get his attention. He finally broke into a canter and bowed his neck from the pressure of the reins.

But both of us had lost our concentration. I knew that Charm sensed my mind wasn't on the exercises—I was thinking about Jacob.

"Working trot, please," Miss Cho said.

I slowed Charm to a trot and tried to collect him. He trotted too fast and it threw him off balance. I couldn't get him on the bit. His trot was flat and he didn't pay attention to my weak and confusing signals.

Ahead of us, Phoenix trotted with balance and

suppleness. He mouthed the bit, listening to Jasmine's every cue. Her eyes didn't shift from looking between his ears. I didn't even look in the direction of the scouts. They'd probably written *She's REALLY on the advanced team?!* by my name.

For the next twenty minutes, Miss Cho asked us for an extended walk and trot, transitions from trotting to cantering and halts. After my ride, I'd be lucky if I got a job leading ponies at Union's county fair.

Miss Cho held up a hand. "Excellent job," she said. "Please line up your horses in the center and wait for our guests to come speak with you."

Charm, with sweat patches darkening his coat, stood between Malibu and Rio. Phoenix stood like gray stone at the end of the line. Jasmine rubbed his neck. Her secret practices had showed in her ride. She'd been near perfect.

The scouts started with Jasmine, but I couldn't hear what they said to her. When their backs were to her, she edged Phoenix forward a step so she could see my face. She smiled and mouthed, "Poor Sasha."

The scouts worked their way down the line. I didn't even listen to them. I'd blown the first round. Charm and I looked as if we hadn't practiced in months. I wished

Heather had never said a word about Jacob. She knew it would make me crazy and I wouldn't be able to . . . *focus*.

"Oh, my God," I whispered aloud.

She'd told me about Jacob—if he was even here—to rattle me before my ride. Heather Fox hadn't changed! She'd been so nice to me for the past couple of weeks . . . she'd tricked me into thinking she wasn't a threat.

"Sasha Silver," said a gray-haired man, consulting his clipboard.

"Yes," I said. "Thank you for watching me ride."

"You seemed to lose focus," one woman said, frowning. "Can we expect better from your jumping round?"

No excuses. "Yes, ma'am. It wasn't my horse's fault. I'm completely focused now and I'll prove it."

The scouts nodded at each other. "Good. Thank you," the first scout said. "We look forward to watching you again."

Mr. Conner stepped over to us. "All right, you may all cool down your horses and wait for your jumping round. Great job."

Yeah. Great job everyone but me. I dismounted and led Charm into the aisle. The final flatwork group headed inside for their ride. A few feet ahead, Heather led Aristocrat up and down the aisle at a slow walk.

"How'd you do?" she asked.

"Awful," I said. "Your plan *totally* worked. Congratulations."

I led Charm away from her.

Heather hurried after me. "Um, what are you talking about?"

"Please. You only told me that Jacob was here to throw me off. You got your wish. I blew my ride."

"Sasha, I'm sorry," Heather said. She moved in front of me. "I told you that because, I don't know, I thought you'd be happy."

"Aw," Jasmine said, cutting in between us. "Sasha, is Heather trying to help you become a decent rider before we jump?"

"Go away," Heather said. "We're just sooo glad we only have to see you until tomorrow."

Jasmine grinned and put a hand over her heart, feigning hurt feelings. "Too bad you're not going to get your way."

"What does that even mean?" Heather asked, looking impatient.

"Guess who's transferring to Canterwood next week?"

Jasmine laughed when she saw the look on our faces.

"I *hated* the idea at first," she said. "Wellington is

obviously the better school. But Mr. Conner is a tough instructor and my old coach was getting soft."

"You're serious," Heather said, blood draining from her face. It wasn't a question, but Jas answered anyway.

"As a heart attack," Jasmine said. "Lucky for you, when I join your advanced team, you'll get to see someone *good* in action. See you later, teammies!" She led Phoenix past us.

Heather and I stared after her.

"I can't—how—" I started.

"No," Heather finished. "Mr. Conner can't let her on the team. She didn't even try out!"

"He won't. There's no way. Then we'd have an extra person on the team."

But we both knew. If he tested her, she'd make it. Mr. Conner would make an allowance.

"Whatever," I said. "She's not on the advanced team today. We are. And she just said all of that now so we'd be distracted before jumping."

"Yeah. You're right. Forget about her. We've got one more round to go."

I sighed. My next round had to be perfect.

"And look—I really didn't mean for that to happen with your ride," Heather said.

"I believe you," I said finally. And actually, I did. The

old Heather wouldn't have bothered to make excuses if she'd really wanted to throw my ride. Plus, I knew she wanted me to do well so we could show Jasmine up.

We started down the aisle and I tried not to think about how much things were going to change after the demo.

33

TOO MANY DISASTERS
TO COUNT

WHEN I GOT OUT TO THE ARENA, I LOOKED for Callie to tell her about my ride, but I couldn't find her. I scanned the stands for Jacob, but didn't see him either. I hoped he'd be back in time for my ride.

Heather's group jumped first, but I was too nervous to watch. Heather came back with a giant smile, though, so she'd obviously done well. She must have known I was concentrating because she bypassed me as she led Aristocrat back to the stable.

You've jumped this course a zillion times, I reminded myself. *You already ruined the first round. If you don't hit this, you're done. The scouts won't consider you at all.*

I took a slow breath in through my nose and let Charm amble around the waiting area. The scouts and Paige sat in the outdoor stands. I didn't see Eric, but Mr. Conner had probably sent him on an errand.

Seconds before it was time for Callie's group, she emerged from nowhere and trotted Jack up to the waiting area. And she'd been worried about *me* being late!

Alison rode first. Her light touch worked for Sunstruck and he made it through with a clean round.

Julia and Trix went next. Trix handled the course like a pro. Julia guided her over the jumps and I held my breath when Trix's back hooves nicked the last rail. But the rail stayed in place and Julia had a clean ride.

Another girl in Callie's group rode and then it was Callie's turn.

Callie and Jack cantered to the first vertical. They made it look easy as they cleared it with room to spare. My eyes shifted up to the stands. Paige clutched her hands as she watched Callie ri—

OMG! There he was.

My eyes stopped on Jacob. He sat at the edge of the bottom row of stands. I stood in the stirrups and waved. I couldn't yell for him and my phone was back in the stable.

Jacob! I screamed in my head. *I'm over here!*

But he didn't even look around. His eyes were on Callie.

He shifted in his seat with each jump. He half-stood when Callie took the final vertical.

Jack thundered over the jump and Jacob grinned. He sat back in his seat, his eyes trailing Callie as she trotted Jack out of the arena.

But that was strange. I mean, he hadn't come to see Callie. He barely even knew her. He'd come to see me, and because he knew she was my friend, he'd politely watched her ride. He just couldn't see me in the crowd of other horses and riders.

Mr. Conner motioned for me to join him, Jasmine, Aaron, and Cole. I tore my eyes away from the stands and forced myself to look at Mr. Conner.

"We randomly drew jumping order," he said. "Sasha, you're first. Then Cole, Aaron, and finally Jasmine. Good luck to all of you."

Cole, Aaron, and Jasmine moved their horses away as I took a breath before starting to the arena. *Jacob's cheering you on. Show him how good you are.*

Mr. Conner put a hand on my boot. "Take your time," he said. "You'll do fine."

"Thanks," I said.

I took a deep breath and urged Charm into a trot. We headed up the slight hill and through the gate of the outdoor arena. I halted Charm once we stepped inside and let him get collected.

I looked over to see Jacob. His seat was empty. I stared at the bench, half expecting him to materialize before my eyes. But he didn't. Why had he left?

Stop and focus! I screamed at myself. *This is ridiculous. In less than two minutes, you can go find him. You've got to get through this round.*

Eight jumps. Eight chances to impress the scouts. I didn't need another second to think about it.

I leaned down by Charm's ears.

"Ready, boy? Let's go!" I kneaded my hands along his neck and he burst into a canter. He headed for the red and white vertical and sailed over it. One down! I let him increase his speed and he lifted into the air and over a black double oxer. The spread didn't even tire Charm and he landed almost gently on the other side. The sooner I got through this, the faster I could find Jacob.

"Good," I whispered. "Next one."

We made a half-turn and approached another vertical. This one was six inches higher than the first. *Three, two, one, and up!* On "up," I squeezed my legs against Charm's sides and he propelled over the rails. He didn't even come close to touching the top rail.

I sneaked a look at the stands . . . still empty.

In the two seconds it took me to look away from the course, Charm had reached a vertical with flowerboxes on the side. He shied away from the fake orange and yellow lilies and tried to run out on the jump.

"No, Charm," I said. I tried to correct my mistake, but it was too late. We approached the vertical before I could get him centered. He jumped awkwardly at an angle. His knees knocked the top rail and it thudded to the ground.

I wanted to stop, dismount and go back to the stable right now. But if I did, Mr. Conner would drag me back to the course and make me finish it. He'd be furious if I quit.

A brisk wind stung my face. Charm tugged on the reins, asking for more, and I let him have another half-inch. The faux wall jump was next and we needed momentum to get over it.

Charm's hoofbeats pounded the dirt. The brick wall loomed in front of us. Charm, not even hesitating this time, launched forward and propelled himself over the wall. I kept myself steady in the saddle and focused on the final jumps.

We were strides away from the second double oxer of the course. The higher rails and wider spread wouldn't have worried me if Charm had been at the top of his game. But his nerves had made him tired and he needed energy to get over the last few jumps.

"Easy, careful," I whispered. At the right second, he flew into the air. But he didn't have enough force. His back hooves ticked the rail and he dragged it down behind us.

I checked him, forcing him to slow his canter, and he eyed the second to last jump, a three and a half foot vertical.

Two knocked rails had shaken his confidence. He cantered with hesitation toward the rails, but managed to get over them. Charm's hooves hit the ground inches away from the jump.

"Last one!" I whispered to him. Charm snorted. He knew what we had to do.

The final vertical had green and gold rails painted in Canterwood's honor. This time, I didn't count strides. I trusted him. When it felt right for both of us, we'd go. Charm kept one ear back—ready to listen to me—and pointed one forward. He cantered up to the jump and we were airborne. Not even close to touching the rail.

We trotted out of the arena and I hopped off his back.

"I'm so sorry, boy," I whispered. "That was all my fault."

I couldn't go find Jacob until Charm was cool. Charm needed to feel okay after our bad rides. I walked him in circles while Jasmine, Aaron, and Cole completed flawless rounds. Jas outperformed everyone in our group. One scout even pointed to her and passed notes to the other scouts.

"You're cool now," I said, feeling Charm's neck. "Let's get you untacked and groomed."

"Sasha?" Mr. Conner asked. He walked up to me. "Let Mike take Charm and come with me for a second."

"Okay," I said, handing Charm's reins to Mike. "He's really tired."

"I'll take care of him," Mike said. "C'mon, big guy, let's get you untacked."

I followed Mr. Conner away from the arena.

"I know I messed up," I said. "I blew it in front of the scouts. They won't even consider me now."

Mr. Conner shook his head. "You did lose concentration, but that happens to even the best riders once in a while. The scouts won't hold one bad demonstration against you."

He was just trying to make me feel better. I knew I'd missed my chance at the YENT.

Mr. Conner led me to a quiet spot by the outdoor wash stalls, where we joined Alison, Julia, Callie, Jasmine, and Heather.

"What's going on?" Heather asked Mr. Conner.

Before he could reply, the silver-haired scout walked over and stood in front of us. He smiled at Mr. Conner and then looked at us.

"Hello, girls. My name is Walt Nicholson—I'm

255

the New England head scout for the Youth Equestrian National Team."

Mr. Nicholson shook each of our hands.

"My fellow scouts and I were quite impressed with your rides today," Mr. Nicholson said. "You've demonstrated tremendous growth since the Junior Equestrian Regionals. That proved to us that you all took this clinic seriously."

Wait. He couldn't be talking to me. Had he seen the parts I'd messed up? The beginning, middle, *and* end?

"Some of the students today struggled with the exercises, but Mr. Conner has told me how you all normally perform. I realize my colleagues and I added tension to the demonstration. Riding under pressure is something you're all working on, correct?"

We nodded.

"Are all of you planning to continue your pursuits of advanced training?" Mr. Nicholson asked.

We all nodded furiously.

Mr. Conner and Mr. Nicholson laughed.

"They are, Walt," Mr. Conner said. "Callie, Sasha, Julia, Heather, and Alison are dedicated riders and students who are among the best in my stable. Jasmine King is also a new addition to Canterwood. She's transferring here next week from Wellington Prep."

Callie, Julia, and Alison turned their heads to look at Jasmine, their mouths open.

"Ah, Wellington," Mr. Nicholson said. "Excellent school. Will Ms. King be joining your advanced team?"

Please say no!

"I'll be testing her over the coming weeks," Mr. Conner said. "If she performs as well as she did today, we'll all be happy to welcome her to the team."

Jasmine smiled angelically at Mr. Conner.

I tried not to roll my eyes. We would *not* welcome her to the team!

"I'd like to come back to watch your seventh-grade advanced team ride again," Mr. Nicholson said. "Over the next several months, my scouts and I will be evaluating riders for the Youth Equestrian National Team. Typically, we like to watch potential members ride three times. We'll be visiting other area schools in June. We cannot guarantee that any of you will make the team as we will be evaluating hundreds of riders who are just as hardworking and talented."

"Does this interest you at all?" Mr. Conner asked us with a smile.

"Definitely," Callie said.

"I'm in," I added.

"So are we," Heather said, looking at Julia and Alison.

"Absolutely," asserted Jasmine.

I almost slumped to the ground in relief that I hadn't blown my chance.

"Good," Mr. Nicholson said. "We'll be in touch with Mr. Conner to set up a date for our next visit. You should be aware that it is the policy of the Youth Equestrian National Team not to offer more than three seats to any school. Often, it's not more than one seat."

Three seats. The six of us looked at each other and then back at Mr. Nicholson.

"Thank you, sir," Heather said.

Mr. Nicholson shook our hands again before Mr. Conner led him in the direction of the parking lot.

"The man must be blind," Jasmine said with a snort. "He's going to watch Sasha ride after she embarrassed herself like that."

"Whatever," I said. "I have to go."

I had to check on Charm and call Jacob to ask him to meet me. Callie and I could celebrate about the demo later.

I started to break away from the group when, over Heather's shoulder, I saw Jacob walking toward us. I beamed at him.

"Oooh, Callie!" Julia said. She jerked her head in Jacob's direction. "There's your boyfriend!"

"*Julia!*" Callie spat.

I turned to look at Julia. "What?" I asked. "He's not Callie's boyfriend."

But you saw the way he watched her ride, a little voice nagged at me. No, Callie would tell me that wasn't true. There had to be an explanation.

"Sure he is," Julia said. "I tried to tell you not to take Callie back. Now you know why."

I looked at Callie, waiting for her to tell me Julia was wrong. Instead, her eyes filled with tears and she reached for my arm.

"Sasha, I've been trying to tell you. But I couldn't! I tried and something always got in the way. I really thought you were with Eric. I never meant for it to happen with Jacob. We started texting and then talking on the phone after the Soirée and——" Callie kept rambling.

I jerked my arm away from her. My head was pounding so hard I could barely hear. "You and Jacob. *Jacob*. And you told Julia?"

"She didn't tell either of us anything," Alison cut in. "But she wasn't good at hiding it. We swiped her phone and read her texts. It was sooo much fun to see how desperate you were to get your BFF back knowing she'd stolen your boyfriend. Sadness."

Heather elbowed Alison. "Shut up," she said. "I didn't know, Sasha." She turned her blue eyes on Callie. "Pretty low, Cal. Aren't you're supposed to be her best *friend*?"

"I'm so sorry," Callie said. "At first, we just started talking because we both missed you and we were upset. But then, we started talking about other things and it wasn't meant like—I mean, I never—I really, really thought you were with Eric. I swear I did!"

"Forget it," I choked out.

Jacob was getting closer with every step and I *really* didn't want to see him.

I turned and ran toward the stable—away from Callie and Jacob. My best friend and my almost-boyfriend. My boots clunked against the concrete as I reached the front of the stable. I pulled open the door and slammed it behind me.

I *knew* Callie had been trying to tell me something. And she'd been so secretive about her texts, but I'd never thought . . . I held back a sob. I'd never even considered that they were from Jacob. But now it all made sense.

I swiped at my eyes, and that's when I slammed into someone.

260

34
IT'S YOU

I LOOKED UP INTO ERIC'S FACE. HE HELD MY arms to steady me and his eyes flickered over my face.

"What's wrong?" he asked. "What happened?"

"Everything!" I wailed. My voice caused a buckskin horse in front of us to pull his head into his stall.

"I'm so sorry I didn't see you after flatwork," Eric said. "Mr. Conner sent me on an errand. What happened on your ride?"

I looked around at the riders working in the stable.

"C'mon," he said. "Let's go by Charm's stall."

I followed him. There wasn't anyone around—this part of the stable was quiet.

"Sit on the tack trunk," he instructed. "Take some deep breaths, Sasha," he soothed. "You're so pale."

I plopped onto the trunk and Eric sat next to me.

"Whatever happened," he said. "I'm sure you tried as hard as you could."

"I didn't," I whispered. "I blew it from the second I started flatwork. Before my ride, Heather came and told me that Jacob was here. I lost all my focus because I was excited that he came to see me."

Eric paused. "Well, at least he showed up. That made you happy, right?"

"But he didn't come to see me." I barely got the words out. "He came for Callie. He's been with her since sometime after the Soirée."

Eric scooted closer to me. "Oh, Sasha. I'm so sorry. She should have told you."

"She says she tried," I said. "I knew something weird was going on, but I never thought it was *that*. She swears she really thought you and I were together. When she finally believed me, it was too late. She was already with Jacob."

I let out a shuddering sigh and hunched forward. Eric started to rub my arm, then he pulled his hand back. He didn't know what to do.

"I should have seen it, but I just *never* thought . . . ugh, she'd been texting him the whole time."

"Jacob should have let you explain," Eric said. He looked really angry, but like he was trying not to look *too* angry. I knew he didn't want to upset me. "And he *definitely* shouldn't have started dating your best friend. I can't believe that guy."

Charm popped his head over the stall door. He strained his neck toward me and his eyes locked on my face. He had the I'm-worried-about-you look.

"I'm fine, boy," I said. I reached over and rubbed his cheek. Charm snorted and kept his head over the door. He always liked to eavesdrop on my conversations.

"I don't want to sound like a jerk," Eric said, "and I'm sorry you got your feelings hurt, but you deserve a better guy than Jacob."

I smiled a wavery smile. "You're a good friend," I told him.

"So, what now?" Eric asked.

"I . . . don't know. I'm *so* mad at Callie. I'm not wasting more energy being upset over Jacob, but Callie and I just got back our friendship. Whatever she believed about you and me, she should have told me about Jacob. He was with me first. She knew it would hurt my feelings. It's best friend *code*!"

"Take a few minutes before you go find her," Eric said. "Stay here and think."

"I will. But what about you? Mr. Conner's probably looking everywhere for you."

"I don't care," Eric said. "I'll tell him the truth—something more important came up."

"You were so great through the whole clinic. I would have gone crazy if you'd been at home."

Eric shifted and turned his body more toward me. "Nah. You would have been fine. But I'm glad I was here, too." He looked down at his hands and then back at me. "And I have to admit, I was relieved that Callie turned me down."

"You were? Why?"

"Honestly? I like someone else," Eric said.

I felt a blush creeping over my face. "You do?"

He nodded. "Since my first day, when she offered to give me directions if I got lost."

Oh, my God. He was talking about me. Eric Rodriguez liked me.

"*Me?*" I blurted out. "You like *me*? Are you sure?"

Eric laughed. "I'm sure."

"But you took Callie's cell number."

"I thought it would help you get your friendship back if I texted her. I just wanted you to be happy."

"Oh," I whispered.

Sweat started to prickle along the small of my back

264

and I tried to figure out what I wanted to say. I didn't even know how to express what I felt. Emotions swirled through me so fast, I felt almost dizzy. Charm, playing chaperone, looked down on us.

Eric had seen me through the Jacob mess, the fights with Callie, and the Belles disaster. He'd been the only one here with me through all of it. I'd been obsessing over Jacob for two weeks, but it was Eric I'd missed when he wasn't around, Eric I turned to when things were confusing or bad. It was never that way with Jacob.

Before I could form words, Eric's eyes locked on mine. He leaned closer and my chest thumped like I'd downed a dozen cappuccinos in five minutes. I'd never been this close to a guy before.

He stopped moving and looked at me, cautiously. "Is this okay?" he asked, brushing a stray lock of hair away from my cheek.

I looked at my lap and then up Eric. For two weeks, I'd been unsure about how to handle everything—Jacob, the Belles, Jasmine, and Callie. But now, for the first time in a while, I knew exactly what to say.

ABOUT THE AUTHOR

TWENTY-TWO-YEAR-OLD JESSICA BURKHART is a former equestrian turned author. When she's not writing books, she freelances for magazines such as *Girls' Life* and *The Writer*. She loves volunteering with Shriners Hospital for Children where she had her own spinal fusion. Visit her website at jessicaburkhart.com for blog entries, "Diary of a Debut Author" vlogs, and more.